Helio Apotheosis

PART 1: THE SCORCHED THIRD

LUKE WOODRUFF
JESSICA SILETZKY, EDITOR

ISBN: 978-1-4834-7936-1 (sc)
ISBN: 978-1-4834-7935-4 (e)

Library of Congress Control Number: 2018900568

Lulu Publishing Services rev. date: 1/15/2018

CONTENTS

or the man I call my best friend, mentor, and father: Andy Woodruff. Thank you for inspiring the words on these pages. The wind is bending the redwoods in Yosemite. I love you, Dad.

PREFACE

he following story is a combination of my own experiences, joys, pains, insecurities, the book of Revelation, and a great deal of imagination. Although it may be loosely based on the book of Revelation, I in no way intend for it to be a prediction of the future. I hope simply to allow those who know Jesus to find peace in the fact that they are not alone in their struggles, and those who don't know Him to discover their need for Him as a savior. Hopefully readers may be touched on the level of the heart and may even be entertained. The fantastical and imaginative have always reached deep into my soul, speaking to me in a language that no other form of artistic expression can. I'd love for my readers to experience just a taste of the joy I have experienced when reading authors like C. S. Lewis, J. R. R Tolkien, Steven Pressfield, and George Macdonald. Thank you and enjoy …

CHAPTER

REGRESSION

I awake to a brown sky, lying on my back. Sitting up slowly, I look around me. Nothing but dust. My hands feel the fine powder beneath me. It's too fine to be sand. Struggling to my feet, I suddenly become aware of the horrible feelings within me, and I immediately despise them. But I cannot name them or their origin. What is my name? I feel as though I've traveled so far, but I don't know where I've come from. I possess a strong urge to get moving, but I don't know which direction to go. Am I cold, or am I hot? All is calm yet full of terror. As far as my eyes can search in all directions, there is nothing but dust. Sharp feelings of abandonment and loneliness begin to grow.

Who has left me?

My stomach seizes and I double over, vomiting clear liquid. I am in agony. Have I known another existence besides this? I cannot remember. I close my eyes and search my mind for memories. A yellow flower. Green grass. Blue. A flash of a woman's smile. I enjoy the feelings that accompany these fragmented memories, but the brief escape makes returning to the pain even more intense. The acute suffering squeezes tears from my eyes. I cry and shake, now ashamed, despite being alone.

The tears actually release some of the pain. I look at my arms and legs and notice I'm wearing weathered brown pants and a long-sleeve brown shirt. The brown boots on my feet match the rest of my clothes, camouflaging my body with the dust beneath me.

Now I must move, so I walk. My legs are heavy, and my lungs burn. A vague memory of the idea that I can walk faster than this is present, but it fails to increase my speed. I walk until the bottoms of my feet hurt and swell within my boots. My throat becomes dry, and the air burns it as I breathe. The need for water consumes every cell of my body. The dust beneath me is soft yet unforgiving to my ankles. My hips begin to hurt. The growing fatigue renders me defenseless to the return of the miserable feelings. Were it not for them, I could run. But they cripple my mind and my body. They are stronger than me. What do they want from me? Endless suffering? Submission? I would submit, if they would leave. But they are my travel companions.

I see something moving. Is it big or small? Close or far? Expecting joy to grow within me, I am struck by the lone presence of fear. The movement gets closer. Shapes of men begin to appear. They are walking in a line, single file, toward me. They suddenly fan out into the shape of a *V.*

Should I hide?

There is nowhere to hide.

Should I run?

Where would I go?

Maybe they have water.

Fear and indecision freeze my body. As they get closer, all except one of them kneel, clutching their wrists, while the standing man raises his left hand. They all wear the same clothes as I do. Each carries a small brown backpack, and each has some kind of small brown device encircling his right wrist. The standing man slowly approaches me. I do not move, as though he will pass me by if I hold still. There are twelve of them. The man approaching me yells something.

I do not understand, so I remain silent.

He yells again, "Did you receive your mark, or was it forced on you?"

This question confuses me. In a raspy voice that surprises me, I answer, "Do you have water?"

The man reaches behind him and throws a brown pouch at me. Keeping his distance, he stands in a ready position, as if preparing to kick a soccer ball. Grabbing the pouch, I quickly untwist the end of it, not knowing how I know how to do this, put the end in my mouth, and squeeze. I drink the water inside until the pouch is empty.

I let out a gasp of air, not realizing I had held my breath while drinking.

The man turns to his companions. "He thirsts."

They all let go of their wrists and stand, seeming to take a posture of ease.

The man walks closer to me. He is tall. My head reaches his chin. I can now see that his face glows a dull light orange. I would have placed him in his forties by the bass sound of his voice and his commanding presence, but his face appears as though he is about twenty—youthful and without blemish. His shoulder-length brown hair is tied back in a ponytail. There are numbers on his forehead. He gets uncomfortably close to me as his glowing red eyes pierce mine. I can feel his presence inside my chest. It's an intimidating yet comforting feeling, as though I am aware of his power but at peace that it will not harm me.

After a few seconds, he turns around and holds up a thumb to his companions. He looks at me again. "Where was your mark forced upon you?"

I am still confused. "I don't understand."

He turns again. "Another one."

Motionless, the men all look at each other, and then at me.

"Do you know who you are?" he asks me.

"No."

My answer brings him closer to me. He gently puts his hand on my shoulder. "You're going to be okay."

A familiar feeling of comfort washes over my painful feelings, like cool water over a burn.

"We'll keep him up front," he orders the men. They fall back into a single file, and he tells me to stay near the front of the line. We begin walking.

As we walk, I notice that the men's faces glow and that each has numbers on his forehead. Each face is youthful and flawless. I feel as if I can see each man's character when his eyes meet mine, even though I've never met them. It's as though they openly share it with me. This is pleasing and comforting.

The walking seems endless, compounding the pain in my legs and feet acutely. It's almost unbearable. One by one throughout the walk, the men turn around as if to check on me, each time responding with a look of disbelief and confusion on their faces. Their postures tell me they are unaffected by the walk. I pour sweat, but I am cold.

My pace slows. The man behind me gently pushes on my back and says, "You can do it."

I cannot. I move out of the line and slow down as the pain overtakes me. The lead man looks back and notices. He holds up his left hand, and the men stop.

He approaches me, handing me another pouch of water and a small tube of a substance that resembles cookie dough when I squeeze it out. The flavor is bland, but my hunger doesn't care. The rest of the men sit in two lines, facing outward, while using the opportunity to eat and drink.

After about five minutes, we are back in line, walking. It takes all of my mental strength to ignore the pain, but I am now able to keep up.

"Time check?" says the lead man as he turns to the man behind him.

"Day 6, hour 18," answers another man.

"Copy."

Before I can ask a question, an aggressive gust of wind howls in the distance. Without speaking, the men move into the shape of a *V* again. They all kneel and grab the devices that encircle their right wrists. The lead man moves forward a few feet, stalking his prey like a lion. He turns around and holds up four fingers. Each man holds up four fingers in answer and stands, letting go of his right wrist.

The man closest turns to me and says, "Stay back, and lie down."

I comply, thankful for any reason to rest. The dust sticks to the sweat on my face. Four men quickly turn around and run backward while the remaining eight run forward. The howling wind gives birth to black swirls of dust. The twelve men form around themselves what look like glowing white cloaks as each man begins floating. The forward men charge through the air.

It's difficult to see, but the swirls of dust take the shapes of unspeakably hideous faces. Each cloaked man flies toward a face. Collisions producing sounds louder than my ears can receive deafen me. I am frozen with fear, surrounded by crashing and shrieks too horrible to describe. I cover my ears, and my eyes close to avoid the flashes of light that each collision produces. I feel a swirl of dust encircling me. My eyes open to see the blackness all around me. The sounds of a thousand screams of torture suddenly fill my head, as each of my limbs moves involuntarily like a snake. I have never been so afraid.

Suddenly, a flash of white light and a terrifying shriek. Everything goes black.

My eyes slowly open as I hear voices. There is leftover terror in my heart and my head, like a bad aftertaste or a festering wound. It's all I can feel. My vision is blurry.

"Tyrus, casualties?" I recognize the lead man's voice. There is commotion all about me.

"Two dead, one out," the man he called Tyrus answers.

"We'll have to take him to a healer," replies the lead man.

I think they are talking about me. The lead man approaches me. "You awake?"

"Yes." I shiver with residual fear.

"Don't worry. It will go away in about an hour."

As my vision returns, I look around and see that many of the men are bleeding bright red from slashes on their faces.

"Who were they?" I ask the closest man as my voice trembles.

"The fallen."

Turning, I can see three men lying on their backs in the dust, faces no longer glowing. The other men are quickly digging two holes with small shovels. I don't know what to do, so I try to stand to help them.

"Just sit down until your shaking stops," Tyrus tells me. He seems to be the second in command. Aside from the lead man, he is the one the men listen to most. He has the same commanding voice and presence that the lead man does, although I can see his submissiveness to the lead man.

"It was trying to fill you, but Zypher stopped it short." He gestures toward the lead man. I thank him by weakly lifting my hand. He just nods as though he had done nothing more than hold a door open for me. My trembling continues as they bury two of the men. Zypher grabs the third man and easily places him over his right shoulder like a sack of potatoes, as though his body is weightless.

"We're moving," declares Zypher.

We quickly form up in a single-file line again and continue walking. After about another four hours of grueling travel, Zypher turns around and asks for a time check again. "Day 7, hour 2," Tyrus answers.

Zypher walks forward, bright red blood dried on his forehead.

He halts the squad with his left hand in the air before placing the man he has been carrying down. He then scans the area slowly, crouching and moving his head like a mounted camera. He then stomps the ground three times. He kneels and says some words in a language I don't understand. The dust on the ground in front of him gives way as a small hole big enough to fit only one body at a time forms in the ground. He gestures for us to enter. The men jump down through the hole one by one as two of the men kneel, flanking the hole and scanning outward. One of them motions quickly for me to follow. Exhausted and unable to think, I blindly follow them.

Once in the hole, we descend on a dust-covered ramp for about an hour, cramped in a dark tunnel only big enough to fit one man in width. We walk in single file. Were it not for the glowing of the men's faces, we would be in pitch black. The imperfections of the tunnel's walls show me that it was carved out.

I would give anything to rest.

We finally arrive in a big open room, like a box about thirty feet cubed. The first thing I notice are seven new men in front of us. Their faces are glowing, and they are dressed like us, each standing in a readied position with a glowing white cloak hovering just above him. I perceive their posturing as a threat. However, I seem to be the only one among us who is afraid. Zypher says something else in his strange language, and one of the men approaches him slowly. He looks closely into Zypher's eyes. Going down the line, he does the same to each of us. As if satisfied by what he has seen, he then raises his hand to the men behind him, and the cloaks above them slowly vanish into the air like water vapor. A large wooden door opens for us, and I am nearly blinded by a brilliant flood of light. It takes a minute for my eyes to adjust.

I see no particular source of the light; it just is.

This room is about ten times the size of the previous room. Shiny dark wood and unique engravings line the walls and ceilings. Commotion is everywhere. There are beds in rows with men and women lying in them with what appear to be doctors attending to various patients. Each wounded person bleeds the same bright red fluid I saw the men bleed after the battle with the swirls of black dust. Women are running back and forth with various medical supplies and pouches of water. People are crying, doctors are giving orders, and people are kneeling beside the beds speaking in strange languages. I see many random doors that lead to unknown places connected by a unifying red-colored floor made of some type of synthetic material. Zypher gently sets down the man he is carrying on the ground. "We have one out!" he shouts as two men quickly grab the man and carry him to a bed.

I find myself collapsed against a wall. The sound of my body hitting the engraved wood has caught Zypher's attention, so he drops to a knee beside me. "This is where healing is done. Stay here. I'll be back." He grabs a man in a white coat and points in my direction. "He was almost filled, but he's okay. Just a little dehydrated … one of the forgotten."

The man nods and steps away for a second. He returns with a ceramic cup full of water and hands it to me.

"Thank you," I say before I drink it quickly.

"You haven't been assigned yet, have you?" he asks. I have no idea what he means and just stare back in confusion. His expression tells me he now understands how lost I really am.

"Don't worry. Someone will fill you in." His attention turns to another patient, and he walks away. As I lay my head back against the wall, my gaze turns upward and I see a huge cross carved into the wood of the ceiling. I don't know what it is, but it awakens feelings so strong that I have trouble breathing. It's as though I'm having a memory that I can't see. I feel terror and nausea crossed with a sense of peace and joy. I become so overwhelmed and exhausted that despite the commotion I fade into unconsciousness.

CHAPTER

REFLECTION

ypher's bass-like voice wakes me up. "You just slept for twenty-four hours."

I'm in a hospital bed in a smaller room full of beds with people like me in them, faces not glowing. There are pictures of waterfalls and mountain ranges on the walls. Some of the people stare catatonically. Others have peaceful looks of relief on their faces, and others have looks of terror and confusion. I see there is an IV in my arm, feeding me some kind of clear liquid. In front of me is a bowl of food with meat and bread in it. The instant I smell it, my entire body is overwhelmed with hunger. I eat the food so fast that's it's gone before I can feel it hit my stomach.

"When's the last time you ate real food?" Zypher asks as he sits beside my bed.

"I don't remember," I say with a mouthful.

"What happened to the other man? The one you carried?"

"The healers are working on him, and it looks like he'll live. He'll be reconnected once his angel has healed."

"Reconnected?"

"Yeah, to his angel. One of the fallen broke the connection on impact. That's why he was out. You'll understand if you get assigned."

"What do you mean, 'assigned'?"

"Once you're ready, you'll be assigned an angel. That way you can fight in both worlds."

The thought of fighting whatever they were fighting earlier flushes my face with fear. He can see my change in demeanor. "Don't worry. You'll be trained first."

The question I'm afraid to ask is, "Why do I have to fight?" I don't want to look weaker than I already must, so I keep my mouth shut. I can see he realizes how overwhelmed I am.

"Don't worry about it now. Just rest."

There are a million questions bombarding my brain, and I can't decide which one to ask first. My mouth opens to speak, and I hear a voice coming through a radio. Zypher reaches into his pocket and pulls out a handheld radio.

"On my way," he says into the radio before quickly leaving.

To the right of me is a woman also lying in a bed like mine, with the most peaceful look on her face. She turns and looks at me. "Have you remembered yet?"

Not knowing what she means but remembering nothing, I answer, "No."

"You will. They can't take soul memory. They thought they could. That's why they did this to us. But they can't. He's in our soul."

"Who is?"

"The Counselor." Her words inspire a sense of warrior-like power in me as she is speaking, which confuses me all the more. I've never met this woman, but it's as if I'm talking to someone I've known since childhood.

"Do you know me?" I ask.

"I know you're one of His. I can see it in your eyes."

"Who is 'He'?

"He's the one who gives all life. He's the one who is behind all love. And He died so we could live."

The feeling of abandonment begins to grow in me again.

"So He's dead?"

"Oh, no. He is very much alive."

I don't understand. "So where is He? And who are we fighting?"

"He's coming back soon. The fight is against the fallen: those who knew Him first and left Him."

Just then Zypher returns. He takes a seat next to my bed with intentional focus on me.

"How are you feeling?" I can tell by his tone that he's asking about more than just my feelings.

"Much better."

"Are you remembering anything yet?"

"No."

"When the fallen one attacked you, did it say anything to you?"

"No. I just heard horrible screams."

"But you're sure you heard no words?" He seems very concerned.

"No. No words."

"The fallen don't usually attack unassigned people so blatantly. Can you remember anything about where and when you got your mark?"

"What mark?"

"Go into the bathroom, and look at your face in the mirror."

It feels as though I've been lying here for days. I stand slowly, aching, and roll my IV stand into the bathroom with me. I feel pressure in my swollen feet with every step. I go into the bathroom with my head down while closing the door. I want whatever my reaction is to be private. I actually don't remember the last time I saw my own reflection. Slowly, I lift my head. My stomach twists, and my breath shortens.

There is a young man before me. Kindness and fear are in his blue eyes. He has short blond hair, cut like a soldier's but slightly grown out. His arms are wiry and muscular. Although his face is young, it is weathered. He appears to be about thirty-five. On his forehead are tattooed in black three numbers. These are the same three numbers that are tattooed on Zypher's forehead and on the foreheads of most of the people I have seen since I woke.

The numbers are 666.

I don't know what they mean or how they got there, but I am instantly nauseous. I don't recognize the man I see before me. He looks like a warrior, but I feel weak, cowardly, and spent. I can't look anymore. I clear the emotion from my face and open the door, making my way back to my bed.

"Any new memories of where you got it?" Zypher asks.

"No." I do my best to hide my shame.

"Well, let me know as soon as you do. It'll give us a better idea of where you come from and what you did before this. That'll help us give you the right assignment."

Maybe this means I don't have to fight.

"You're gonna have to get dressed and come with me. The injured need these beds."

A nurse hands me my clothes, clean and folded. I go back to the bathroom to change. Zypher knocks on the door.

"We gotta go," he says through the door.

"Roger," I answer instinctively. Why did I say that? I follow him through a few doors and hallways, back into the chaos where we first entered. He stops in the middle of the large room, and he raises his hand, index finger extended, and makes a circular motion. Out of the madness emerge all the men we were with earlier, plus two new additions, both with glowing orange faces. Zypher addresses them. "Fill-ins?"

"Yes, sir," they answer, in sync.

They both glance at me with confused looks on their faces, as though someone had brought a child to battle.

Zypher extends his right hand and shakes each of theirs. "Don't worry about him. He'll keep up."

I will? I think to myself.

"Call me Zypher. And your names?"

"Apollo."

"Zuriel."

They look nervous.

"You both came highly recommended. You ready for a fight?"

"Definitely, sir."

"Oh, yeah." Their eyes light up.

"Good. Let's head out."

We exit through a different way than we entered. We go up a few staircases and then climb a ladder that goes up a couple hundred feet into a dark, narrow tunnel. My legs are rebelling. We arrive at a circular passage door like a manhole cover with a combination lock on it. Zypher places his hand on it until it glows red. The cover opens like the lid of a teapot. In single file, we climb about another hundred feet and come to another combo lock cover. Zypher opens it, and I can see the brown sky again. We climb out one at a time, and I see each man crawling on his belly as he reaches the dusty surface. I do the same. Zuriel is crawling next to me, and he whispers, "We have to do this for about a mile so we don't give away our exit. Friggin' sucks, but it's for safety."

I appreciate the heads-up.

The dust is harder and sharper than it looks. Even though I'm wearing a thick shirt, my elbows are bleeding after about an hour of crawling. The frustration of not knowing where we are going, combined with the pain in my elbows, amplifies my growing impatience.

"Where are we going?" I finally ask Zuriel.

"Quiet!" snaps Zypher.

We continue to crawl in silence. Subconsciously I have fallen into their *V*-shaped formation. The dust is unforgiving. I can now see blood seeping through the elbows of my shirt. Dust clings to the sweat on my face and hands. After what feels like four hours, Zypher motions for everyone to stand up. We are now walking in the *V*. Zypher, next to the tip of the *V*, raises a fist in the air. Without thinking, I freeze. All the other men freeze as well. No one moves or speaks for about two minutes. I can feel myself breathing steadily. Through the dust I see a shape manifest in the distance. It moves toward us. Zypher turns and holds up three fingers. All the men hold up three fingers in answer and then turn a dial on the metal attachments on their wrists. Zuriel comes over to me. "Lie down and stay put. Watch the rear, and holler if you see anything. This will be over pretty quick."

I obey. Zypher extends his right arm, and a white bolt shoots from his wrist weapon. All the men begin doing the same in the direction of whatever was moving toward us. Eight of the men drop to the ground on their stomachs and continue firing, while four of them sprint forward and dive on the ground. Then four of the men who were lying down quickly get up, sprint forward, and dive back on the ground. After a few seconds, they continue this pattern but as individuals. Each man who is lying down fires, while a man next to him sprints forward, and then hits the ground and begins shooting. Their movement as a whole is flawless and strangely beautiful and somehow very familiar to me. As a unit, they look like a snake slithering sideways in the sand, advancing toward whatever I saw in the distance. Every few seconds, I see a flash go over my head like a small lightning bolt passing over me. I lose sight of them, and I am left alone.

After a minute or so the shooting stops. Zuriel returns and beckons me. I get up and follow him. We walk for a bit, and I see the men all standing around a large brown cluster. As I get closer, I see that it is a pile of dead men, each of them riddled with charred holes. Apollo is dragging a body, and he effortlessly throws it on top of the pile.

"Unassigned fallen," Zuriel tells me.

"How did you know?" I ask.

"None of our people enter this way, and none had exited for hours."

There are six dead men, each with the same "666" mark on his forehead. Surprisingly, the sight of the dead bodies doesn't bother me.

"Why did Zypher hold up three fingers?" I ask Zuriel.

"The three means third-dimension warfare."

"Okay, light 'em up!" Commands Zypher.

Apollo pulls a small bottle out of his pack and pours a clear gel all over the bodies. Then he lights the pile with a match. The bodies are ablaze instantly. The smell is unbearable. I can almost taste it. The stench is so foul that vomit is pouring from my mouth before I can cover my nose.

"Yummy," mocks Apollo.

Zuriel and Apollo look at each other and embrace, patting each other on the back. All the men begin embracing one another in the same way. Zuriel comes over to me and gives me a powerful hug, squeezing all the air out of me.

"We all made it. Thank God."

I take this to be a celebration of no life lost on our side.

Even though the smell caused me to regurgitate, it is familiar to me. It brings up feelings of loss that I'm trying to place in the darkness of my lost memory.

Zypher motions for us to keep moving. We quickly form back into our *V* and continue walking. I look back at the black smoke billowing into the sky, charred corpses beneath it.

The men walk very slowly when in a *V* formation, so slowly that it hurts. The journey seems to never end.

Where are we going? Who am I? I hate knowing so little.

We walk at this pace for hours. Finally we stop.

"We sleep here," Zypher declares.

Each man pulls a small, thin sack out of his pack and spreads it on the ground. Zypher hands me an extra. "It's warmer than it looks," he assures me.

He also hands me a plastic tube filled with the same kind of cookie dough-like substance as the last one he gave me. Despite the bland taste, it fills me up. I end up lying next to Zuriel. This is the first time I've had a chance to stop moving since I left the healing bed.

"So what's your name?" he asks.

"I don't know."

"Don't worry. You'll remember. All the saved remember."

His face glows like the rest of them. I take the opportunity to ask, "Why do your faces glow?"

"Our assigned angels make them glow." He can see my confusion. He continues, "Each of us is assigned an angel who follows us everywhere. Their presence and our connection to them create the light."

He interlaces his hands together, demonstrating the tether between him and his angel.

"You'll be assigned one as soon as we know where to put you. But I have a feeling Zypher already knows."

We both look at Zypher. He is sitting on his sleep sack, looking at the horizon as if on watch. Zuriel turns back to me.

"You look like you know how to move in formation. Do you have memories of fighting?"

"I don't really have any memories."

"In time ..."

He looks young, but as for the rest of them, I cannot place his age. Although I know he is a warrior, his face has the innocence of a child's. It's a contradiction all the men possess. Their bodies look as though made of steel, even though they are flesh. I look at my own body and see a resemblance.

"Where do our marks come from, the ones on our foreheads?" I ask.

"It's the mark of trade. Before the war began, it was required in order to trade anything. Some people received it willingly as the king's decree. Others, like us, had it forced upon them."

I begin to question myself.

"How do you know mine was forced upon me?"

"Because we recognize the saved through their eyes. And you have human traits. Those men we killed earlier—they received their marks willingly."

"What makes me one of the 'saved'?"

"You belong to Him."

He must be talking about the same man the woman in the healing room was talking about. Tears are welling up in my eyes, but I don't know why.

"Who?"

"The Prince Himself. Jesus the Christ."

I know the name. I know it like I know I'm alive. I know it so intimately that I long to embrace Him but don't know where He is. A rush of emotions overtake me so powerful that I begin sobbing uncontrollably.

"Is he remembering?" asks Zypher, turning toward us.

"Looks like it," answers Zuriel.

I begin spouting out questions I don't understand.

"Where is He? Why has He left me? Does He know I'm still alive?"

The questions are pouring out of me faster than the tears. My words flow effortlessly from my mouth, and I don't know what I'm asking until I hear myself ask it.

"I know it feels like He's gone, but He's not."

Zuriel puts a comforting arm on my shoulder.

"We have a battle to fight, and in the end He will win it for us. But until then, it is our lot to fight."

The fear is growing in me again.

"How do we fight without Him?"

"We are never without Him."

I am trembling. I'm still trying to make sense of my emotions as the men fall asleep one by one. Zuriel stays with me for another few minutes in silence just to make sure I'm all right.

"I've got first watch. You'll be all right. Just breathe through it," he tells me as he gets up and leaves. I'm left shaking and aching in my sleep sack. After about an hour, exhaustion takes me under.

THE FALLEN PRINCE

slowly wake to the sting of the cold burning my face. My feet and toes feel frozen even under socks and my sleep sack. My whole body feels heavy, like gravity has twice the strength that it normally does. My eyelids are so heavy that it takes all of my concentration to lift them. I would simply go back to sleep, but an overwhelming need to urinate compels me to get up. It's a miserable process. I feel like I'm going to piss myself, but my feet feel like they're made of concrete, and I'm shivering uncontrollably. I randomly stumble out into the dust, not feeling like I'm far enough away from camp to go yet, so I keep going and keep going, increasing my speed, hoping I'll warm up in the process. I finally feel far enough away and relieve myself just in time.

When I'm finished, I turn around and can see only pitch black. I walk in different directions, faster and faster. The realization that I am lost sparks panic. I'm afraid the cold will kill me if I don't find my sleep sack soon. After a couple of minutes, I see a dim light in the distance. It must be one of the assigned. I quickly move toward it, and as I get closer, the light gets brighter and brighter, much too bright to be an assigned man. There is a figure within the glow that beckons me. I'm afraid but strangely drawn to its welcoming presence. I can now see that the figure is a young man. His face is young and without blemish. He has golden shoulder-length hair and wears a white robe.

"Welcome," he says, with the most gentle voice I've ever heard. He extends a hand to me.

"We've all missed you, and now you're home."

"Do you know me?" I ask, hoping that he does.

"Of course I know you, my child. I've been watching you since birth."

He looks into my eyes. "Do you feel forsaken? He who has abandoned you should never have done so. I, however, will never abandon you."

I have felt it since the moment I awoke. But this man eases my unrest. I take his hand. It is warm to the touch. I look down and see that his hand is beginning to change color. Starting in his fingertips, the light is snuffed out by a blackness that is creeping up his arm. The warmth is gone, and his hand turns to ice. My heart is overtaken by fear. His grip is so strong now that it's crushing my hand. The pain drops me to a knee.

"And now you're all mine." His voice gets deeper with this declaration.

The instant the words leave his mouth, I see a brilliant flash before my eyes and hear a shriek. I'm blinded and deafened for a second, but when I regain my vision I see a man's body with a black wolf's head, snarling and drooling. Then there are two more flashes and sounds of an epic collision. Two men stumble backward after colliding with the wolf creature. He looks angry but unharmed. I turn around and see all of the assigned squad, glowing in white light and charging the wolf-man. A flurry of collisions ensue. I duck my head and plug my ears as my senses are overloaded. Men lay strewn about the ground, crawling and stumbling. Finally Zypher arrives, glowing in red light. He charges the creature at full speed, flying through the air like an arrow. This collision has a lower pitch to it, and the shock wave from it knocks me over. It takes me a minute to regain my bearings, and the first thing I hear are muffled voices.

"He's gone." It's Zypher. Thank God he's alive.

"*Casualties?*" he yells, sounding disoriented.

"Four out!" answers Tyrus. "But they're conscious!"

"Good. Let's get them moving. He may be back soon with more."

All the men fall into single-file formation and start jogging. We come upon our sleep sacks, and then men grab them and pack them on the move. I end up behind Zypher in formation.

"What was that?" I ask him between heavy breaths.

"The prince of the fallen of this entire region. Why he would attack an unassigned is a mystery to me though. He has thousands of men to do that for him."

He is clearly disturbed. He turns around and looks deep into my eyes.

"Who *are* you?" He has a challenging tone in his voice.

"I told you I don't know."

"Well, you're staying with me from now on. If a prince would attack you, you must have been somebody really dangerous to the enemy."

"How were you able to fight him off when no one else could?"

"I've been assigned a captain."

"But—"

I start to ask another question, and he hushes me. I can only assume that he's still a little shaken and has a lot on his mind, so I stay quiet.

The men are moving at a rapid pace. I surprise myself by being able to keep up. Maybe I just needed some food and sleep. A little pride wells up within me. But I am instantly deflated as fear sets in at the idea of the possibility of another fight on our journey.

For the next few hours, I forget that I'm walking in a wasteland and spend most of the time thinking about this Jesus. The name is familiar, so I search the dark corners of my lost memories to find more information. Perhaps he's my Father. I know He has somehow saved me, as I recognize my deep feelings of gratitude and love for this man. I realize he's more than a prince; he's a king. He somehow comforts me emotionally, physically, and mentally. Amidst the deep connection I feel, I am also haunted by the fact that I don't know where He is or when He's coming back. Frustrated, I push the thoughts from my mind.

The remainder of our journey goes uninterrupted. We spend four days walking and four nights sleeping on the ground, the men taking turns staying up and keeping watch. The monotonous sight of endless dust begins to blur my senses. I see no other signs of life or varied terrain for days.

One of the nights as we get ready to sleep, I end up next to a man named Simeon. He was formerly assigned, but he hasn't glowed since the battle with the prince. His connection with his angel has been broken, making him one of the "out." To look at him I would think him a farmer. His demeanor is calm, and his movements are slow and deliberate. Since he no longer glows, I can place his age at about forty-five. I take another opportunity to gain information.

"Why is there nothing but dust? Where are the plants, the animals?"

He looks up at me and slowly raises his brow.

"Well … the dust is because the Father scorched the Earth. There is life, but not much here on the scorched third."

"Scorched third?"

"Yeah … the Father scorched a third of the Earth. And that's where we are. You must have been a brave man to end up here unassigned, or just unlucky."

I appreciate the respect he shows me as he speaks to me. All of the men have been treating me differently since the fallen prince attacked me. Before, it was as though I were an annoying child along for the trip, and now they speak to me as a man. They are more aware of the circumstantial significance than I am. But I feel like I'm being given respect I didn't earn, so I try not to get too familiar.

"Thank you for fighting the prince for me. I know it cost you your connection."

"You're welcome, but I was just doing what my assignment called for. I'm betting you've done greater things to be singled out by a prince."

The gash from the collision on the side of his face is wide. It has the color of dry human blood, no longer the bright red color I saw before.

"Get some sleep; you'll need it," he tells me before going to sleep himself.

The next day is the longest. By the end of the day even Zypher's pace begins to slow. Even though I carry only water, my back aches terribly. My feet are so swollen that I can feel my pulse in my boots. Each beat of my heart stings my feet. But all this pain is becoming more and more familiar to me, almost as though I were at home with it. Just when I think I can't take another step, a mountain range begins to reveal itself in the distance. For about the next three hours, we walk as the mountains seem to maintain their distance. I'm starting to think they aren't real.

I cannot continue, but I must.

After we stop for a short water-and-snack break, the mountains finally start to grow in size. As we get closer, they grow so tall that I have to bend my neck to see the top of them. They are covered in dust like the rest of the land. The mountains resemble large fingers, adjacent to one another. We start our climb in between two of the "fingers." Now the hard part begins. Every step is misery. My feet sink into the dust, and it seems to take five steps to move one foot. It's almost as though my soul aches now, and not just my body. We finally reach a ridgeline. All of my muscles are on fire. I welcome the downhill walk that follows.

After a few hundred feet, Zypher gives the signal to stop. Like before, he stomps on the ground. The dust then gives way, and a hole forms. One by one the men jump in. I follow. The fall is about ten feet. My weak legs buckle on impact. Pushing myself up and dusting off my pants, I look up to see a great iron door in a room that is barely big enough for all thirteen of us. Zypher kicks the door three times. A six-inch-wide slot opens, and Zypher presses his face close to the crevice.

"How many?" I hear from the other side of the door.

"Four out, eight assigned, one unassigned," answers Zypher.

"Let's see," the voice commands.

Each man sticks his eyes up to the slot.

"Clear," I hear after each one.

Apollo motions for me to go next after he is cleared. I am very nervous as I put my eyes up to the slot. I'm waiting for what feels like a whole minute. I'm startled by the charging of a wrist weapon. "Open your eyes, please."

I didn't realize they were closed, so I quickly open them.

"Clear."

The door loudly unbolts and groans open. I see the fading of white cloaks in the air as we enter. Seven glowing men are recovering from their readied stances, turning the dials on their wrist weapons to uncharge them. Zypher and the lead man of the seven embrace.

"Zorien, how you doin', douche bag?"

"Let's leave your mom out of this," the man answers.

They share a chuckle, and we all go through a smaller door that leads to myriad hallways, all lined with some kind of shiny, dark green stone. We pass by several small doors, and each man enters one.

"You four out. Come with me." Zorien motions for them

to follow him down the hall. Zypher points to a closed door and looks at me. "That's you. I'll come get you in the morning. Tomorrow, we see what you're made of. Sleep well; you're gonna need it."

He leaves me with that.

Entering my room, I am surprised by its size. It's bigger than I expected. There is a small bathroom with a shower in the rear, a twin bed, all made, and a light bulb in the center of the ceiling.

"Better than sleeping in the dust," I mutter to myself. A warm bed is about the most welcoming thing I could ask for at this moment. Sitting on the bed is a clean and folded replica of what I am wearing. After a refreshing shower, I get under the covers and am instantly asleep.

TRIALS

In the morning I am awakened, not by any noise, but by a powerful presence standing over me. I open my eyes, and the sight of Zypher standing over my bed completely still is a little unnerving. He is cleaned up and in clean clothes, alert and awake.

"Let's go. Get dressed, and come down to breakfast. Your assessment starts today. I don't know how you've done what you've done, but hopefully we can find out today."

I had no idea that I had done anything. I quickly get dressed and then follow some men through hallways and down stairs who tell me that they are headed to breakfast. Apparently, word about the incident with the prince has spread, because men are looking at me and whispering to each other as they see me pass. A small, skinny, very energetic, friendly-looking man approaches as if we know each other, and he begins walking alongside me.

"Are you the unassigned who came in just last night?" He has an energy that keeps him bouncing slightly as he walks.

"Yeah."

He is unassigned as well. His head is freshly shaved, and I would guess him to be about twenty-one. "I'm supposed to get mine soon. Almost done testing. I hope it's a seraphim. They said I did good on the combat testing, plus my dad was assigned a seraphim. You know they're the warriors, right?"

He seems very eager to impress me.

"Oh, I'm James, by the way. I heard you kept up with a squad of elite assigned. I didn't even know an unassigned *existed* who could do that!"

He talks so fast I can't get a word in.

"Kept up? I didn't even fight."

"No, I mean on the trek. You didn't fall out and kept up with their pace, right? Everyone's talking about it. Plus, I heard you got attacked by a prince, bro! Wicked! How'd you survive that one?"

"Zypher saved—"

"I can't wait to get out there! All right … anyway … nice to meet you, bro." He abruptly ends our conversation and walks ahead of me.

I enter through some green double doors into a large cafeteria filled with men and women, assigned and unassigned. I spot Zypher, and he waves me to his table. My food is on a tray already waiting for me. I'm delighted at the sight of meat and eggs. I sit and eat without saying a word. There's also a freshly cut apple and a glass of grape juice on my tray. I devour my meal as Zypher and the other men sit in silence. I notice that the four out men are at the table but glow once again.

"You done?" Zypher asks when my food is gone. I burp loudly without trying.

"Guess so." He continues with his bearing intact, "All right, so today begins your assessment. It's where we find out what your strengths and weaknesses are so we know which class of angel to assign you. Now, my men have scheduled training, but I've allowed them to skip it because they all want to watch your assessment. As a matter of fact, the whole camp is curious to see how it goes."

The pressure is on.

"After breakfast you're gonna take some tests. Then we'll start with combat."

I was afraid he was going to say that.

"Okay." I try to pretend like I'm not afraid.

My breakfast has barely begun to digest before Zypher takes me to the first of a series of different rooms. I'm given a full physical, I take a bunch of math and reading tests, and I play with shapes and puzzles while talking to a psychiatrist. I find it all very tiring. The men in Zypher's squad all follow me, eager to know my scores after each test. I don't know what the scores mean as each tester gives them to me on a printed sheet of paper, but the men seem impressed each time. When I finish with the final math test, Zypher looks at me with anticipation.

"All right, let's go to the fight room."

My fatigue turns to nerves as I feel a small surge of adrenaline. I follow him to a room filled with wrestling mats. The rest of the squad is close behind, all chuckling to one another and looking at each other as though they share some inside joke that I'm unaware of. There is an older man in a jogging outfit and a younger, very in-shape blond girl waiting for us. I can't help but notice how beautiful she is.

"Let's get to it," says the older man. All the other men get into a circle surrounding the blond girl and me. I am confused.

"What are we doing?" I ask.

"You're going to fight Christine here," the old man tells me with a smile.

"What? No, I'm not."

"Well, then you're gonna take one hell of a beating."

Without hesitation the girl charges me and hits me with a front kick right in the balls. I double over in pain and collapse to my knees. *"Ooohhh!"* The men all holler.

"You'd better get up, princess. She's waiting!"

The old man is starting to get on my nerves.

I stand back up but refuse to fight. She charges me again with the same kick, but this time I instinctually block it. She throws a flurry of quick punches, all of which I dodge, surprising myself. I side stepher and bear-hug her, not letting her move. She stomps on my foot, which really hurts, but I hold fast to my grip.

"That's enough," declares the old man. "You passed."

I let loose my grip. "I what?"

"You didn't' hit her. You passed. Well done," he says as he leaves in a hurry.

Christine turns around and gives me a friendly hug.

"You know how to treat a lady. Sorry about the crotch shot."

She winks at me, and she leaves. At this point, I'm just angry.

"What kind of sick game was that?" I ask Zypher.

He laughs. "Calm down, buddy—just a test of character. Next comes the real combat testing."

The old man returns with an unassigned man about twice my size. His arms look like ham hocks, and his legs resemble tree trunks. He doesn't stop staring at me from the moment he enters the room. He wears shorts and a tank top, so I can only assume he's here to fight me.

"Okay, this is ridiculous. I have to protest," I say.

"Just do your best. We'll stop it if it goes too far," says Zypher.

"Oh, very comforting." My sarcasm doesn't help my situation.

The men circle up again, all with smiles on their faces. Without hesitation the big man charges me. I freeze for a second, but then without thinking I throw a quick overhand right, hitting him in the chest. He collapses, holding his chest and wheezing. The old man kneels down to help him. The men all stare at me, mouths ajar. I'm as surprised as they are. Zypher looks at Apollo.

"You're up," he tells him. Apollo gives me a look of apology and then reluctantly removes his jacket.

"Nothing personal," he tells me.

Apollo and I are about the same size, so I'm not too worried at this point, considering what I just did. The old man helps the big man out of the room as he mad-dogs me. With my inflating ego I turn back toward Apollo. I get into a fighting stance, and I begin bouncing around the room thinking, *This will be fun.*

This time I charge and throw a few hooks. Apollo sidesteps and catches one of my punches, moving faster than I've ever seen a human move. I try to muscle out of the hold, but his strength is overwhelming. I feel as though my elbow's about to snap, so I instinctually tap his leg, indicating my submission. He lets me go and then comes at me and starts throwing punches and kicks faster than I can block them. A kick hits my leg, and I crumple to the ground. As soon as my knee touches the ground, I see a fist, hear a thud, and see a flash. Then blackness.

I wake up on my back. Zypher is kneeling over me. "He's awake. All right, one more time."

I don't realize that he means we are to fight again. "One more what?"

"Quit screwing around. You were doing all right; you just dropped your guard for a second."

Now I remember. I stand up and face Apollo, much less confident this time. Without warning he comes at me. I actually block his first few punches and return a few of my own. He pauses for a second, shocked that I was able to hit him. Bright red fluid begins to drip from his nose. He quickly touches it and looks at his fingertips. He then looks over at Zypher, who is equally in shock. They both look at me, and before I have time to react Apollo hits me square in the stomach with a side kick. I collapse and can't breathe.

"Okay, that'll do." Zypher's words are a welcome relief to me. He helps me to my feet.

"We've never seen an unassigned draw blood from an assigned before. That was incredible."

I try to smile at the compliment, but my face is still grimacing in pain. I can only breathe shallowly, and every breath hurts for about the next five minutes. I try to play it off as the men each pat me on the shoulder, leaving the room. I'm left with Zypher. "You all right? There's a lot more to go."

"Yeah, I'm good," I say in a weak voice. He chuckles.

"You've got about fifteen minutes before the fire-and-movement course. Catch your breath, and get some water."

And here I was hoping it was all done. Although I am a bit more confident having surprised myself with abilities I didn't know I had, I'm actually curious at this point to see what else I can do.

I sit in a white chair in a hallway, sipping water from a pouch when Zypher and the squad return with various looks on their faces. A couple of the men look a little annoyed, as though I had taken something from them. A couple others look excited with anticipation. And Zypher looks unreadable, steady as usual.

"Ready?"

"Oh, yeah."

But I'm suddenly nervous again. The silence of the men as we walk down the shiny green hallway is unsettling. We continue down two flights of granite stairs, and finally into a large, warehouse-sized room. The walls are brown stone and are covered in scuff marks and small, round indents. About twenty assigned men are waiting there for us. There are all kinds of obstacles, like six-foot walls, six-inch-high steps, tall narrow columns, and concrete spheres as tall as a man. I look up and I can see dozens of glowing faces through plate-glass windows, all staring down at me. The audience is clearly there for me.

The men waiting in the room are in red military dress uniforms, with multiple diamond-shaped chrome emblems on their shoulders. They stand with their arms behind their backs, all staring at me and whispering things to one another. I have no idea what I'm supposed to do. Zypher hands me a brown clamp that resembles the devices that the men wear around their wrists.

He can see that I don't know what to do with it, so he clamps it around my right wrist. He turns a dial on the device, and it makes a sound as though it's charging.

"Don't move your fingers on this hand yet. Your goal is to get through the course while hitting those targets, without getting knocked out." He points to several bull's-eye targets on the far wall, about three hundred yards away.

"Knocked out? By what?" I ask, now not even sure I want to do this.

"Projectiles." He points up toward the far wall, where I now notice mini-cannons all pointing down at the course. Zypher puts a black turtle shell-like helmet on my head, and I can see that there are scuff marks and miniature cracks all over it. Very reassuring.

"To fire, point and flex your two middle fingers twice very quickly. Good luck."

He begins to walk away as the men clear the floor.

"Wait!" I stop him.

"What?"

I have nothing to say.

"Don't worry. It's just training."

"Thanks. I feel so much better," I mumble under my breath.

Zypher points to a red circle on the floor behind the first obstacle that says "start" in it. Then he gives me a thumbs-up. I hesitantly walk to the circle, and I wait as the men go up staircases that lead to the area behind the plate-glass windows upstairs. All the doors close, and I'm left alone in the large room. A gentle female voice comes over the loudspeaker.

"Begin in ten, nine, eight…"

I look up to try to find Zypher through the plate glass. I don't know what to do. I take aim at one of the targets and wait for the countdown to finish. I figure I'll just open fire as soon as I hear "zero." I notice some frantic motion in the corner of my eye and look up. Zypher and the squad are waving at me trying to tell me something. I hold my hands up as if to ask what.

"five, four, three …"

At "three" the lights go out. At "zero" I hear a dull thud and then am instantly on the ground. I can't see, but I can feel the blood coming out of my mouth. I crawl and feel my way behind a wall. I sit with my back against the wall, and I can feel a strong impact against the wall every couple seconds. This goes on for a minute or so as I let my vision adjust.

I am dizzy, and I can feel blood running down my chin. I can't just sit here. Quickly, I peek my head around the corner and retract it. Something whizzes past my head. I do it again. Another whiz. Without pause I do it again. Nothing. Okay, they can only fire every couple seconds. I do it twice more and then get up and sprint to the next cover, which I can dully see is a two-foot-tall-by-three-foot-wide step. I dive behind it as something strikes my calf. I growl in pain. Crouching behind the wall, I can feel my leg throbbing. I see on the ground next to me what hit me. I pick it up and see that it's a small wooden ball about the size of a walnut. No wonder that it hurt so much. Pain in my elbows is now growing. I hit them pretty hard when I dove on the floor, which feels like sand-covered concrete. I can feel the impact of the projectiles against my cover. The rhythm has now quickened.

I suddenly remember I'm supposed to be shooting at something.

I listen to the rhythm of fire again and peek my head out between shots. I can barely see the outline of the targets on the wall, let alone the center. I peek my head out again, and this time I notice a small blink of a light in the center of one of the targets. I look a few more times just to make sure I'm not seeing things. On one of my looks, my ear gets clipped by a projectile. The stinging throbs on the entire right side of my head. Fortunately, I noticed some blips of the blinking red light in the center of a few of the targets. They're quick and sporadic, but they are there. I bring my right hand up to my chest and get ready to fire. When I hear my chance in between shots, I quickly expose half my body, arm extended. I focus in on the front side tip of my wrist weapon, making the target blurry. Flexing my two middle fingers twice rapidly like Zypher said, I am surprised by a flash from my wrist. I then see an explosion and fireworks. Direct hit. I forget that I am exposed and get tagged right in the thigh. The pain drops me, and I roll behind cover again.

I can't believe I hit it.

My body's reactions to these tests are surprising me. It takes me a minute to recover from the hit to the leg, and I gather by the continuing barrage of projectiles that I'm not done. I now have the fire's rhythm down and successfully sprint to the next covered position. I time my next shot, and I take out another target, and then another one. I take out the last target, and the gentle voice sounds off again.

"All targets destroyed."

I sit with a sigh of relief with my back to a wall, still bleeding from my mouth. I look up through the plate-glass windows and see all the men just standing still and staring at me in disbelief. I search for Zypher. There's a huge part of me that cares about only his reaction. I find him and meet his gaze. He nods slightly, and then tilts his head and lightly shrugs his shoulders as if to say, Not the worst thing I've ever seen. Coming from him, that's good enough for me.

Two men in brown jumpsuits quickly come out of a side door, carrying medical bags. They attend to my wounds and give me water. As my adrenaline settles down, the pain really sets in. While drinking water from a pouch, my tongue notices something isn't right. I run it across the entire row of my upper teeth and am shocked when I realize both my front teeth are missing. One of the medics sees this and goes to the start of the course to find them. Zypher comes down the staircase and walks up to me.

"Looks like you're gonna need dentures. Ha!"

The medic returns with my two front teeth in a plastic baggy.

"Don't worry. We'll have them reattached," Zypher reassures me.

The rest of the squad approaches me. Tyrus takes my hand and helps me up. "Well, we at least know you're getting a seraphim!"

"Tomorrow you'll be assigned after they weigh your scores." Zypher gestures with his chin to the men in red uniforms upstairs. Several of them are looking down at me, taking notes on clipboards.

"They're all trying to get dibs on you for their battalions. Only problem is, they assume high test scores mean you're a good leader."

Zypher stares at me for a second. "That remains to be seen."

He walks away. Any feeling that he was starting to become my friend has just been put in check.

I spend the rest of the day in oral surgery, having my teeth reattached by a man in a white coat using some kind of tool that looks like a soldering iron. It burns terribly. He talks to me about a cabin he used to own in the woods before the war started, and all the fishing he used to do. It's actually a nice escape from the present pain to hear of such things.

The next morning I'm awoken again by Zypher's presence standing over me. "It's that time," he states matter-of-factly. "Meet me back here after breakfast."

I can hardly eat, as my stomach is full of even more anxiety than it was the day before. I know my testing is done, but the idea of having an angel as my companion and having to take place in the kind of fighting I've seen is just too much to think about. Do I know the first thing about fourth-dimension combat? I still don't even know who I am. I don't finish my breakfast, and I head back to my room. Zypher is already waiting for me.

"You ready?" He gives me a half-cocked smile.

"Not sure," I answer, surprised by my own honesty.

"Don't worry. This is the easy part. All you have to do is listen. Follow me."

He leads me through hallways and down staircases for about fifteen minutes. I'm wondering where the rest of the squad is. We go through some large double doors, and I see high on the wall a life-sized engraved wooden cross with a man hanging on it. The mixed feelings of nausea and peace return. But the peace overtakes the nausea within a few seconds. The room is filled with pews, and the floor is a beautiful white stone tile. There are engravings in the wooden walls of a man suffering in various ways. There is one of Him being whipped, another of Him carrying a cross, and another of Him being nailed to a cross by Roman soldiers. There is a crown of thorns on His head, and the thorns have cut into His head, making blood run down His face. I somehow know that these pictures represent the Jesus whom I've been thinking about so much. I remember that these are the sufferings He underwent for me. Zypher sits in one of the pews and gestures for me to join him.

I sit down, and memories begin to flood my heart and mind. I'm a child again in church, singing to God with all my might. Tears run down my face. I am in heaven. I am now aware of my connection with Him and His love for me. It is eternal and unknowable. My capacity to understand love is as full as it can get, and His love overflows that understanding. I am His. I will fight for Him. I will die for Him. I long to see Him and hear Him.

I come back to reality and see Zypher quietly waiting, sympathizing with my reactions. "Take your time. They can wait a few minutes."

When the tears clear from my eyes, I can see the familiar Bibles in the backs of the pews. The scenes on the wall bring back memories of stories from the gospels. My mind is flooding with story after story from this book. I've known the scripture since

I was a child! I'm remembering that I had parents, and brothers and sisters. My heart breaks as I relive separating from them at age twelve.

I joined the fight shortly after that.

I've been in the fight for many years. I've killed many fallen, and I can see their black eyes flash through my mind. I was in charge of my own squad of unassigned warriors doing elite missions. I've lost men under my charge. I can see their faces, and I know each of their names.

I was captured in my last mission, and my mark was tattooed on my forehead while I was strapped to a table. I can still see the lifeless black eyes of the fallen as they ruthlessly tortured me for information. I'm still haunted by their indifference.

This flurry of memories is all too much, but I want more. I'm remembering who I am, or at least who I was. I can smell rain, and I can taste sugar and salt. What's my name? I can hear my mother say it.

"Lucien." That's it.

My name is Lucien.

"Lucien!" I hear myself say out loud.

"What?" asks Zypher, startled.

"Lucien. It's my name!"

"Oh, yeah?"

Zypher begins to guide me. "Take them in slowly. Don't let them overwhelm you. Savor the good ones. See the bad ones, but don't dwell on them. Let them pass. When we're done here today, you'll have some time to sit down and write everything down so you can piece it all together. But in the meantime, let's get you assigned."

I shake my head to clear it, and I stand up. I follow him into a small, cozy room where the rest of the squad is already waiting for us. They are seated in a half circle on the ground. A man in a purple linen robe with a glowing white cloak floating over him is standing in the middle. I take a bit of a defensive posture, but Zypher puts his hand on my shoulder. "It's okay; his angel is a priest angel. They can fight, but their main purpose is holy ceremony and prayer. Have a seat."

Although the priest is assigned, he appears to be about forty. He has small wrinkles at the corners of his eyes that are exaggerated by the friendly smile he wears. His kind presence is soothing. The room is lined with light gray fabric, and the floor is soft blue carpet. There's a small table off to the side with a coffeemaker brewing fresh coffee and a small brown box filled with little white cakes. The smell of the coffee is intoxicating. The priest notices me eyeing the rich, dark liquid.

"Would you like a cup, son?"

"Yes sir."

I wait, not knowing if I should serve myself. The priest raises his eyebrows and looks at me.

"Well? I'm not a waiter. Go ahead." He chuckles.

The rest of the squad laughs. I sheepishly make myself a cup in one of the Styrofoam cups that are on the table. The rest of them men line up behind me to make cups of their own. Oh, they were waiting for me to go first.

We all sit, sipping coffee while they talk and laugh over the experiences of the last few days. They include me in their discussions.

"And you knew he'd never been attacked by a demon before when you saw the look on his face."

Tyrus points at me, laughing.

"Don't sweat it, junior. I pissed my pants the first time I was attacked. Literally."

That is a little reassuring.

"So you're doing better than me already."

"My first time I ran into a lake, thinking I could wash it off," Zypher says, laughing.

During our discussions Zypher rarely speaks. But when he does, all the men are silent and give him their full attention. He spends most of the time sitting back with a pleased look on his face, like a father who is happy that his children are getting along. It's good to see him enjoying himself.

"All right," says the priest as the conversation has died down. "Let's get down to business."

He looks at me.

"We are here to assign you an angel. He will be your companion in battle—especially fourth-dimension battles, where we humans are powerless alone. An angel is a gift to each of the saved from the holy Father." He changes his tone. "Now, we won't force an angel on you. There are plenty of jobs for the unassigned. There is no shame in working a support job."

I feel exactly that: shame that I am even considering it. But knowing now what I know of the Father, I gather that He has specific plans for me.

"Your scores have been weighed son, and I gotta say, they're pretty well up there. Everyone in the camp is talking about it. You've got a gift, and it's your responsibility as one of the saved to use it for good. Seeing what you've seen and knowing what you know, do you accept assignment?"

I clench my fists and ignore my doubt. "Yes, sir."

Did I just say that? I didn't even think about it. How much of that was to avoid shame, and how much was because it was the right thing to do? It is too late to think about that now.

"Glad to hear you say that, son. Didn't wanna say it before, but it would be a waste of a gift to keep you in the rear." The priest throws a glance at Zypher, whose bearing makes him impossible to read. The priest seems to understand him though. "So, we've determined that you will be assigned a seraphim. They are the warrior class. Your angel's name is Octavian. We can't pronounce his real name, but he's the first to be assigned from the elite eighth legion. Hence the name Octavian."

I'm thinking, *Okay, great! Where is he?*

"Now let's pray." Everyone bows their heads in unison. I

follow suit. "Our Father, who is in heaven, hallowed be your name. Your kingdom come, Your will be done, on Earth as it is in heaven. Give us this day our daily bread. Forgive us our trespasses as we forgive those who trespass against us. Lead us not into temptation, but deliver us from evil. Lord Jesus, we have before us a willing warrior who belongs to You. He has fear as we all have fear. But he has courage."

I am hoping what he is saying about me is true.

"We pray that You will clothe him with the power of the Holy Spirit and assign him the holy warrior Octavian as his battle companion. We pray that You will bless their time in battle and protect their connection. We pray all of this in Your precious name, Lord Jesus. Amen."

I open my eyes and see that the priest is clothed in the glowing white cloak that was hovering above him. It slowly fades and then disappears off his body. I expect something to happen, but nothing does.

"What now?" I ask the priest.

"We wait. Sometimes the Father says no."

Now I'm nervous again. If the Father discovers how scared I am, He will definitely say no. But He must already know. He knows my heart and my mind even before I do. So why would He say yes? I'm sure that He wants fearless warriors, not insecure ones.

Before I can beat myself up further, I start to feel weightless. I'm floating off the ground, but I can't feel what is lifting me. My face is getting very hot. All the men are looking at me with looks of pride, as though I were a four-year-old riding a bike for the first time. I try to speak. I can't. I start to flail and panic.

"Whoa, whoa. Relax. Let it happen," the priest says.

I try to calm down and stop struggling. My whole body is warming up. I watch myself rotate my arms and wiggle my legs. I look around the room, and whatever I focus on becomes clearer than I've ever been able to see. My vision zooms in like binoculars at will. As I'm floating, I'm rotating upside down, so I kick at the air to try to make myself upright again. Clearly I don't have the hang of this yet. The priest tells me to close my eyes and relax every muscle in my body. I do, and slowly my body corrects itself, and I return to the ground.

"That helps to give you more control," he instructs.

Once I'm back on the ground, I look down at my hands. Sure enough, they glow with the same orange light that the rest of the squad glows with. Not only can I see the glow, but I can feel it. It's like a gentle heat circulating through every vein in my body. It's as though I've been cold my entire life and finally found warmth. I'm beaming with excitement.

"Don't get too happy. We still have to train you to fight with him," says Zypher.

The priest stands. "Well, gents, my work here is done."

He comes over to me. "May God bless you in the fight, son."

"Thank you, sir," I say, honored.

I can see Zypher say some words to Tyrus, who then turns to the squad. "All right, fellas, back to work."

They all stand and go with him. I'm left with Zypher.

"It's pretty obvious you used to be some kind of warrior," he says.

I haven't told him all I remember yet.

"But whatever fight you were in was only in the third dimension. Fourth-dimension combat is a whole new beast. They can get in your head and torment you to no end. They can injure your angel and break the connection, leaving you vulnerable to attack or even death. But sometimes they just prefer to torture you because the taste of it is so sweet to them." Zypher pauses as if to shake off a bad memory. "What you got on that first day was only a taste. Some men are driven mad by it and either kill themselves or have to spend years in a padded room. Are you ready for that kind of risk?"

I don't want to disappoint him, but I don't want to lie to him either. "I don't know, but that scares me."

I'm surprised how easy it is to be totally honest with him.

"It scares me too," he relates. "But never forget that no matter what, we will be with Him in the end. All this fighting is only temporary. Good work over the last few days. Go ahead and take the rest of the day to get used to this. And remember, you're a lot stronger now, so be careful." He leaves me to find my own way back to my room.

At lunch I'm lost in thought about who I used to be. Some of the memories are still jumbled, and I'm piecing them together. I remember being in charge of a group of men during several firefights against the men with black eyes. I remember intense elite training, and how I was taught to use weapons of all kinds. My father was a leader in the church and joined the resistance when the mark started to populate. I see him die. I feel a tear roll down my cheek.

But my mind doesn't stop. I remember the plagues striking the Earth, the news reports about the land being scorched, the flying scorpions and men screaming, and the awful slaughter. The screams of the men are still in my head, like a symphony of suffering. I remember thinking it would never end.

As I force myself to be in the present, an abstract memory persists. It is a strong feeling of fear. But it's more than that. It's fear I ignored—fear I surrendered in the fight. Fear didn't stop me from fighting.

I return to reality for a second and notice that my metal fork has been crushed in my hand. I do have to be careful. I look up and see a man sitting across from me, observing my behavior. I can see that he is unassigned.

"Just got assigned?" he asks.

"Yeah, still getting used to the strength. I'm Lucien, by the way. When are you getting assigned?"

"David. Nice to meet you." He hesitantly extends his hand,

obviously averse to his hand ending up like my fork. "No, I chose not to be assigned."

He retrieves his hand, grateful it is intact. "I'm more gifted working with equipment than fighting on the front lines. Besides, I've seen enough death to last two lifetimes. I used to fight with the resistance when the emperor started trying to wipe out the saved."

"The emperor?"

"Yeah, the beast. You were one of the forgotten, weren't you? And your memory is still returning?"

I nod.

"Wow, they usually don't assign someone so soon. You must be a special one."

He rubs the hand I shook as though he doesn't need to hide that it hurts a little. "I was one of the forgotten, but I've had my memory back for a few years."

"How did we lose our memories?" I'm suddenly very interested. "And how did I end up in this scorched third all alone?"

"They left me there too. Luckily, a squad of assigned saved picked me up. Those of us who were captured had the mark put on us; then we had our memories wiped and were left alone in various places. They thought that if our minds had no memory of belonging to Jesus, then we would no longer belong to Him. But they didn't count on the concept of soul memory."

"Soul memory?" I interject.

"Yeah, soul memory. Even if our brains were wiped clean, our souls, which are really the essence of us, would know that we were saved. Were you met by a squad of assigned saved shortly after you woke up?"

"Yeah, I was."

"And were you attacked shortly after that?"

"Yeah, how do you know this?" I'm starting to talk over him.

"Those fallen angels were supposed to pick you up shortly

after you woke up. They must have been late. So they probably tried to kill your squad so they could fill your mind first and try to recruit you, making you believe that you belonged to the fallen all along."

I pause for a moment. "And what happens to those they do meet with before any saved get to them?"

"Well, they've recently been discovering that they buy into the lie for a while, but eventually soul memory takes over and they rebel."

He takes a deep breath. "They've been rounding them up and executing them publicly by the hundreds. But the rebellion doesn't stop them from continuing the experiment. What gives us hope is that the forgotten who are executed go to be with the Father, and we will see them again soon."

The gruesome memories of the executions begin to flood my brain. My heart is breaking as I'm now remembering my older brothers dying in battle when I was a child, and watching my mother and sisters being executed on television. I was a warrior without a family. I fought recklessly. I had nothing left to lose. Overwhelming feelings of anger and vengeance are taking over.

I see David talking in front of me, but I can't hear him.

Now I know why I fought fearlessly. Rage. I killed out of anger to feed revenge.

I am bursting and need to act out, or I will explode.

Abruptly I stand up and let out a deep scream of sadness and anger. My fist comes down on the table and splits it in two, like snapping a twig. The whole cafeteria goes silent. I realize what I've done and see the hundreds of eyes on me. David has leaped back and is trembling. Sheepishly and quickly I leave the cafeteria and go to my room. It's not until I lie down that I realize how exhausted my body is from the whole assignment process. I escape into a deep sleep.

CHAPTER

OCTAVIAN

find myself in a forest, walking alone and at peace. The smell of the air is crisp and pure. I'm surrounded by beautiful, majestic redwoods swaying in the wind. They tower into the sky and surround me like older, wiser companions.

I look up and can hear gusts of wind coming from a distance, and as they get closer, I see the tops of the redwoods gently bend, giving in to the power of the wind. I continue walking when a man appears beside me. I am not startled. Somehow, I just knew he was there the whole time. He greets me.

"Hey."

I nod my head and smile.

"This is so beautiful, isn't it, Lucien?"

"Indeed."

The man appears to be in his forties. He wears a red flannel shirt and blue jeans with brown hiking boots. He has shoulder-length blond hair with a beard to match. His voice has a gentleness that mimics the atmosphere of the forest.

"So, I'm looking forward to our time together," he says. Without introduction, I know that I'm speaking to Octavian.

"So am I. Thanks for taking this assignment."

"Hey, it's an honor. I've been watching you for some time. I'm sure there are many men after the Father's own heart, but you're only the second one I've ever heard Him say by name."

Simultaneously feeling beyond honored and equally beyond inadequate, I'm sure he's got the wrong guy.

"Believe me, I'm talking about you, Lucien."

Apparently, he can read my thoughts. He continues, "Our God does not make mistakes. You're not the bravest or the wisest or even the smartest guy on Earth, but you have a passion to love and belong to the Father that is purer than most. And that's what makes Him smile. But don't let it get to your head. You fall short in many other ways. If you didn't, you wouldn't need the grace of the Son, Jesus."

Well, that's convicting.

"So what's next?" I ask.

"Well, you've got some training to do. As you thought earlier, you know nothing about fourth-dimension combat."

I don't know if I like the fact that he can read my thoughts.

"Don't worry. Your secrets are safe with me. What should worry you is that the enemy can read your thoughts too. But they can also hear your prayers, which should worry them. Another part of my job is to fight the fallen that desire to attack your mind. You may not have known it, but they've been in your head many times, dating all the way back to your childhood. The absence of this confusion and spiritual static will make you a better warrior. But don't think that I can always fight them all off. They will get in there sometimes, and that's when it's up to you to pray and just rely on Him."

"So how do I fight with you against the fallen?"

"Well, it's hard to explain and will take some practice, but it involves a great deal of concentration to 'think with the soul,' so to speak. Although your physical body is involved to some degree, try to think of that part of it as the steering wheel, and your soul and myself as the car."

I look at him vacantly. He tries again. "It's like as souls we interlock arms and charge the enemy. But it's all about momentum advantage. We have to strike first. If the enemy is gaining more momentum than us and we collide, you could be killed, or I could be seriously injured, breaking our connection. If our connection is broken, you become 'out,' or just like an unassigned again. In that case, I would have to return to the Father for healing and could be gone for days, weeks, or even months. But if our momentum is greater before a collision with one of the fallen, then we send them into the abyss. The exception is if we are fighting a prince. He needs almost no momentum to defeat us, and even charging him could be suicide ..."

I am suddenly aware of the risk the men took for me in fighting that prince.

"...unless you've been assigned a captain. Then you can fight a prince; hence what you saw Zypher do. But even then, he just retreated; he wasn't sent to the abyss. Sending a prince to the abyss is not an easy task. Anyway, you'll learn more tomorrow."

We stop and he turns to me. "Now, I know this forest is nice, but it's time to wake up. Zypher has something important to talk to you about."

I sit up in my bed, not feeling sleepy at all. Zypher is sitting in a chair in my room, looking at me. I'm a little less startled this time but still taken aback.

"You gotta stop doing that," I tell him.

He laughs. "But your reactions are priceless."

"Well, I'm glad you're entertained."

For about thirty seconds, there's an uncomfortable silence.

"So what's on the agenda today?" I ask just to break the silence.

"I need to talk to you about something important."

Just like Octavian said. I cut him off. "I think my angel was in my dream last night. He mentioned this—"

"Yeah, he'll visit from time to time. I'd take notes when I woke up if I were you, Lucien. Anyway, I did some research on you. It turns out you were quite the warrior for the resistance." He leans forward in his chair, resting on his elbows. "It also turns out you were quite brutal."

"How so?" I ask.

"Well, you would torture the enemies in pretty horrific ways when you captured them. You even had to stand trial for it. Lucien, what do you know about our enemies that are human?"

"I'm not sure." I'm lying. I think they're permanently lost vermin that need to be exterminated.

"Well, the humans, especially the unassigned, are not completely fallen from grace."

"What do you mean?" I already knew that.

"Well, I mean that if they are captured, it's not our policy to kill them or torture them. Ever." He is looking at me with great intensity. "They can still repent and be saved. And if you know anything about the Father, you know that His love and forgiveness are never spent, even on them."

I do know this but am too ashamed to admit it, given what I've done.

"Don't get me wrong. In a fight I will take them out to spare my men, but I will also save them if I can. Lucien, I know what happened to your family, and I'm sorry for that. Believe me when I say that I understand fighting from a place of rage. But you have to know that revenge is a monster that can never be fed enough. As a matter of fact, it's something that the enemy would cultivate in us, even at the loss of his own men, because it makes us more like him. We must not feed it. We have to fight from a sense of love for our people and duty to the Father. We fight for each other, not to satisfy our anger. If you don't understand this, then you shouldn't be on the front lines."

He is very stern with me. He can see my shame.

"We've all done what makes us undeserving. I just want to make sure your heart is ready for this. Anyway, we're working on getting you a unit to join. The higher-ups are still debating where you should go."

"You mean I'm not going with you?"

"We're an elite squad. It takes a lot of training and field experience to join an elite squad. You have to be selected."

The idea of having to go into battle without Zypher is terrifying.

"Well, how do I get selected?"

"You have to spend time in a line unit for a while. Hey, you've got the skills to be elite; you just need the fourth-dimension experience, that's all."

As if that were some minor detail.

"Besides, my squad is full," he says with finality. He stands to leave, and then stops and looks at me. "Think about what I said."

The door closes behind him. I'm left for the rest of the night to ponder my fate.

The next morning, I wake before Zypher has a chance to hover over me. When he comes into my room, he's surprised to see me dressed and blousing my boots.

"Let's go."

I follow him into the cafeteria, where I get looks from all sorts of glowing faces and red eyes. The looks make me feel as though I've done something wrong. I see Zypher's squad, and I am comforted by their familiarity. The first person I greet is Apollo. He ignores me. Tyrus stands with a huge smile on his face, and he gives me a firm handshake. "Great work, bro. Have a seat. Relax."

I look back over at Apollo, wondering why he is ignoring me. He just shakes his head, looking disappointed. I try to play it off, but I can definitely feel tension at the table. Most of the squad ignore my presence. Zypher looks at the squad one by one.

"The decision is final, so just accept it. Tyrus, fill him in." Zypher gets up and leaves.

"Fill me in on what?"

He hesitates and then looks at me with a grin. "You're with us now."

"What?" I am pleasantly shocked. "How? I mean, don't I need experience since you guys are elite?"

"You would think so," snaps Apollo with a sarcastic tone before getting up and leaving. That stings a little, but I'm too happy to let it upset me.

Tyrus continues, "Well, the higher-ups wanted to give you your own platoon in a line unit based on your scores, but Zypher convinced them that you would get men killed. The only way they would change their minds was if Zypher took you in his squad."

I'm too relieved to let that bother me. Besides, he's probably right.

"We've got a mission in a couple days, so we have some time to do a little 4D training." He tells me that like it will put my fears to rest.

After lunch, Tyrus takes me to a large, empty room. Black canvas lines the walls, and the ceiling is blue like the sky used to be.

"What are we gonna do here?" I ask.

"4D sparring," he says with a smile. "Okay, now I want you to tell Octavian with your mind that it's time to fight. He knows this is only sparring, so he and my angel won't allow us to hurt each other."

Not quite sure how to use my mind to talk, I close my eyes and speak with my internal voice, saying, "Octavian, it's time to fight."

Warm light appears above me. There is a glowing white cloak.

"There you go! That's him, getting ready for battle."

I look at Tyrus, and I see that his cloak has already wrapped itself around him.

"Now, as soon as your feet leave the ground, he will encircle you. Then it's a matter of using your soul-thinking to guide him."

"Soul-thinking?"

"Yeah. Use your heart to guide your direction."

It sounds ridiculous.

I jump in the air, and I am immediately supported by white light. It feels uncomfortable to be floating, like I'm trying to stand on a baseball with one foot. As soon as the feeling of nervousness kicks in, I begin vibrating and then bouncing around the room, hitting walls and slamming on the floor.

"Calm your emotions! Close your eyes for a second, and think peaceful thoughts."

I think about a waterfall. This makes me hold still.

"Okay, good. Now, instead of thinking about going left or right, *desire* to go left or right."

I'm not sure what this means, but I give it a shot. Nothing.

"I don't desire to go any direction."

"Okay, try this: Trust that you have a need to go a certain direction. Don't logically ask yourself 'why?' Just know it in your heart."

Again, I'm not sure what this means, but I try to take my mind out of it. I simply believe that I have a need to go forward. I move forward through the air in a jerking manner, like a car with its clutch being let go too fast.

"That's a start. Now do it without so much tension in your body."

I try to relax my body while holding on to the need. My movement smooths out.

"Good. Now inject some fire and passion into the feeling."

This attempt only results in more tension and jerky movement. This trial and error clumsily continues for about two hours. I am impressed with Tyrus's patience. I have small moments of improvement, but I always end up where I started.

At lunch I'm so tired I can hardly bring my hand to my mouth to feed myself. Tyrus sees this and chuckles. I don't feel any particular muscle soreness or fatigue; it's more like a general lack of communication with my body.

"Why am I so tired? I didn't even use my body."

"Yeah, but you wore out your soul. And you can't disconnect the body from the soul."

He recites it like he's said it a hundred times before.

"Make sure you finish all your food, or you'll be even more exhausted when we spar."

"We're not done?"

I don't feel like I could train another minute, let alone spar with a highly trained elite warrior.

"Don't worry. You'll still be alive tomorrow," he says, almost with amusement.

In that moment, I realize my training is on an accelerated path. I'm wondering if hidden behind his patience and smile is a secret agenda to show my incompetence.

After lunch I drag myself back to the training room, and I have trouble even communicating with Octavian once I get there.

"Why can't I just ask Octavian to move one way or the other once I'm in the air?"

"It doesn't work that way. Besides, your connection to him isn't that deep yet. You have to go through some battles together; then you'll be able to communicate more clearly. Okay, once you're in the air, I want you to come at me."

I finally have Octavian above me. I leap up off the ground, and I am floating. With all my will and passion I charge Tyrus, taking out all my frustrations of the day on this single charge. He simply moves through the air to his left, and I collide with the wall. This knocks the wind out of me and drops me to the ground.

"Good effort, but too much anger. Passion is great, but anger clouds your aim. It's only natural that you're pissed, but control it. Get up. Let's go again."

I stand up, wheezing.

"What are you waiting for? Christmas?"

I jump in the air and charge him again. He comes right at me, and we collide. I find myself on the ground, feeling like I hit the wall again. Now my body aches.

"Better, but now you need to work on being aware of your opponent's momentum. If it's greater than yours, avoid the collision. If it's not, you can win the fight. Didn't Octavian talk to you?"

"Yeah," I whisper in pain.

"Well, how 'bout listening then? Let's go. We're not done." His patience is thinning.

The thought of another collision makes me want to cry, but I know I have to earn respect if I want to stay in this squad, so I get up. This time, I charge in a way that feels lazy to me because I'm so exhausted, but I find myself going faster than before. I have no sense of how fast Tyrus is coming at me, but I continue straight regardless. We collide, and all I see is a flash. I'm wincing in preparation for pain, but I feel none. I open my eyes and see Tyrus on the ground, smiling up at me.

"There you go!" He quickly stands, unharmed. "Now, do you know why it worked that time? Because you were so tired that you were able to relax your body and just think with your soul. But you need to be able to do that all the time, or we'll be burying you in the dust. Okay, great work. I know you're tired, but make sure you get some dinner. Then we're having a meeting about our mission."

I fall asleep at dinner about five times. Tyrus keeps nudging me to wake me up. I'm so exhausted I don't even have a sense of how the squad feels about the progress of my training. I don't even care. I just want to sleep.

At the meeting Zypher is drawing formations and locations on a whiteboard. My eyes are so heavy that it takes all my concentration just to not fall asleep. I have none left to pay attention.

"Lucien!" Zypher snaps at me.

Uh-oh.

"What time are we returning to base?"

"Uhhh … I'm not sure."

"Go stand in the back, and pay attention! If you don't know this mission, you could get someone killed."

"Yes, sir."

"My name is Zypher, not sir. Now wake up," he growls at me. "We're returning to base at day 3, hour 2 from departure."

"Roger."

Now that the adrenaline of being embarrassed is running through my veins, I stay awake. I get the gist of the mission. We're leaving in two days, and we're attacking an outpost of assigned fallen ones who are holding twenty-three unassigned saved scheduled for execution.

Back in my room I take notes of as much as I can remember about the mission. There are some holes that I need filled in because I dozed off during the briefing, which scares me because I'll have to ask someone. I can hardly sleep thinking about all that could go wrong. I almost wish something would go wrong to postpone it. I don't feel ready. I just got the hang of moving with Octavian. Fighting experienced fallen is a different story.

Over the next couple of days, training with Tyrus is trial and error. He pushes me to limits I didn't know I had. I've been pushed to physical limits in training before, but spiritual limits involve a whole new kind of pain for me. When you're spiritually exhausted, your perception of everything is skewed. Your concept of time goes away. Any physical pain becomes numbness and seems insignificant.

A day before the mission, I'm training with Tyrus, wiped out beyond what I've ever known.

"How am I going to fight tomorrow if I'm exhausted?" I ask.

"Don't think about it. You're tougher than you realize. Besides, we all know that 4D is new to you, so we'll be watching your back," Tyrus responds.

He's trying to put me at ease, but I feel like I'll be a burden to the squad. However, I'm still thankful to be with them rather than be in charge of a whole platoon.

CHAPTER

SALVATION

trangely enough, I sleep well that night. I wake up not even remembering what lies ahead. Tyrus walks into my room, and it all comes flooding back. All my muscles start tensing up.

"Let's go. We gotta eat breakfast before we get out there."

I'm hardly able to eat breakfast. Although I've been on my share of missions, I know this one is different. I feel like it's my first mission all over again. Zypher goes over various key points of the mission while we eat. He goes around the table asking questions to test and refresh our knowledge.

"Lucien, how many suspected assigned fallen are we facing?"

"Two squads, approximately twelve."

The fallen travel in squads of six.

"Right."

At least I knew that one.

Within thirty minutes of finishing breakfast, we're all at a staging area, checking our gear and wrist weapons. Tyrus reminds me not to be a hero and to keep in mind that this is a combination of 3D and 4D warfare. I'm confident with 3D at least.

Before I know it, we're climbing a ladder that leads to another manhole with a combo cover on it. We go through a couple of these and come out at the base of the mountain, low-crawling. We low-crawl on our bellies in our *V* formation for about an hour, and then we get up and begin walking. Zypher motions for us to get into single file, and we really start stepping it out. With minimal breaks, this goes on for the rest of the day. Now that I'm assigned, this is a piece of cake. I feel like I don't even need rest. We still stop to sleep for about four hours; then we continue.

Halfway through the second day, I see something on the horizon. I realize I can see much farther now. It looks like rolling hills just starting to take shape. There is movement, but it's so far away that I can't see what it is. Zypher motions us all to the ground. I'm suddenly painfully aware that my mind is going blank, and I can't remember my part in this mission. I wait for someone to make a move that will give me a cue. Before we get the chance, impact rounds are striking the ground all around us. One of them skims my shoulder, which stings terribly. They must have seen us coming. I look down at my shoulder and see bright red blood pooling near my clavicle. I can now see men firing at us in the distance. Instinctually I hit the ground and start returning fire. I fall into the rhythm with my four-man team of sprinting, hitting the ground, firing, getting up, sprinting … I've hit two men already, dropping them instantly.

As we get closer, I can see more and more bodies coming out of holes in the bases of the rolling hills. Many of them are dropping as soon as they surface. A few of them are now floating, cloaked in black dust. I freeze when I see this.

"Four!" shouts Zypher. All of the men in my squad are now floating as their angels appear.

"*What are you waiting for?*" Tyrus shouts at me. "Get your ass in the air!"

I snap out of it and focus. I find I can float, and Octavian appears more quickly than he ever has in training. He must know this is not a drill. I look up and see a black bolt headed toward me at lightning speed. I barely have time to move out of its way. Once again I am surrounded by collisions and shrieks. I see a black bolt just miss Apollo. I immediately charge it. The collision and following shriek is so loud that it makes me go temporarily deaf.

I'm still effortlessly floating, and I see a lifeless body with black eyes lying in the dust beneath me. This is my first 4D kill. I don't have time to consider the dead man before I'm hit from the side by a demon that knocks me to the ground. Miraculously, I'm still alive and Octavian is still with me. But blood now drips into my eyes from a wound on my forehead. The assigned fallen man stands over me with lifeless black eyes. He looks indifferent, as though I were a piece of trash that he's deciding whether to pick up and throw away or not. His black glow intensifies as his feet leave the ground. He charges me to finish me off. I roll to the side just in time as he collides with the ground, leaving a two-foot-deep crater where I was. I can't focus enough to counterattack, so I fire some 3D shots into his chest. They knock him off balance long enough for me to charge him, killing him instantly and sending his demon into the abyss with a pitiful shriek.

Each shriek I hear makes my heart ache with sorrow, as though I wish I could have saved the poor lost soul that just departed. Yet I have to keep fighting. The next several minutes are chaos. I react only instinctually, and I am singularly aware of each moment as I experience it, not the one before or the one to come. I find myself wrapped up in a wrestling match with one of the assigned fallen after we collide with equal momentum. His strength surpasses mine. I stick my fist into his gut and fire several shots. This weakens his grip on me but doesn't stop him. He now has a vice grip on my throat with one of his hands. I can feel my windpipe closing, and I am unable to breathe. Suddenly, my white glow grows in intensity, snuffing out the black surrounding him. I feel his strength lessen, and I am able to snap his arm in two with one strike of my fist. I can only assume Octavian had something to do with it. He drops to a knee, screaming and holding his arm. I finish him off by crushing his skull with a solid left hook to the side of his head.

The last couple of shrieks die down, and I hear Zypher's expected question, *"Casualties?"*

"Two out!" answers Tyrus.

I look around and see Apollo sitting on the ground, staring off into nothing, blood covering his face, no longer glowing. I go over to him and offer my hand. He looks up at me, surprised, but he reluctantly accepts. I help him to his feet, and I can see that he has a small limp.

"You two stay out here and watch the perimeter. The rest of you come with me inside," orders Zypher. I can only assume he thinks there is no more danger on the surface, so he leaves the two least capable men to keep watch.

The other man who is out is named Spero. He's separated from his angel but is physically intact, so he follows the rest of the squad into an opening at the base of one of the hills. Apollo limps his way in between two of the small hills and lies facedown. He looks back at me and motions for me to keep an eye out in the opposite direction.

"If I need 4D help, I'll yell for it," he tells me.

"Roger."

I lie down prone and face the opposite direction, keeping a lookout. I wait for what seems like ten minutes. Then I hear a muffled series of shots, collisions, shrieks, and Zypher yelling orders. I want so badly to go in and help, but I know I have to stay put. After about five minutes of the noise, there is sudden and complete silence. I wait in anticipation for a sign that the squad has been victorious. Finally, I hear Zypher's voice. I can't understand him, but the fact that he's alive tells me that the enemy is dead. He comes out first, with an unassigned civilian over one shoulder. As the squad follows behind, two more of the men are carrying unassigned civilians. Mixed among the squad are very frightened-looking unassigned people. They are all pale and tired-looking. I count about thirty of them.

"Guess twenty-three was just an estimate," I say under my breath.

Zypher sets the man he's carrying on the ground and begins CPR. The man is young, maybe eighteen at the most. After a few minutes Zypher stops, looks at Tyrus, and slowly shakes his head. "Let's hurry up and bury him."

Two of the three men carrying unassigned manage to revive them. One is a young woman, about twenty, and another is an elderly woman, about sixty-five. The third person is a middle-aged man that they quickly begin digging a shallow grave for. Something about the deaths of these people hits me harder than the previous deaths I've seen. I try to hide my sorrow, as I know this is not the time for it. I start checking the unassigned people, making sure they are okay to move. They all seem pretty shaken but can walk. I give each of them some water as the rest of the squad finishes burying the two dead men.

"Let's move!" says Zypher.

I try to explain to the unassigned in the gentlest way possible that they have to walk with us for the next few days in the dust. They all start asking me questions about loved ones, family members, times, locations ... I have no answers for them, and I urge them to get moving before more of the fallen arrive.

"We managed to disable their radios before they could get a message out, but we should still get moving," Zypher tells me.

Since the unassigned are so slow, Apollo can keep up, even with his limp. We have to give up most of our own food and water along the way to sustain them. We brought extra in anticipation of this need, but we could carry only so much. Many of them, especially the elderly, need to stop for frequent breaks. I am impressed by the patience of the squad. Zypher takes time with all the people as we walk, asking them about their experiences. He approaches a young woman walking near me, so I can hear their conversation.

"So where are you from?" His voice is gentler than I've ever heard it.

"Idaho." She keeps her head down. It takes everything in me not to think of what they may have done to her.

"Do you remember how long you were in there?"

"No, they keep us drugged so we can't escape or give any information if we do."

"Yeah, I know. Do you remember getting captured?"

"I just want to know where my family is."

"And we'll work on that when we get back. But anything you can tell me will really help."

"Okay." She pushes herself to elaborate. "Well, we were all in church one day when they came in. There were about twenty of them, all covered in glowing black cloaks. They said we were in violation of the worship laws and put us all in trucks. Once we got to the holding cells, they separated us, and I never saw any of my friends that I was arrested with after that. The only thing I remember about being here is a lot of questions from the fallen. They would ask us where churches were … then … hurt us … then ask us again. I only knew where my church was, so they hurt me a lot."

She crosses her arms across her stomach.

"I'm so sorry you had to go through that. But you're safe now. And we'll never let them hurt you again. What's your name?"

"Tabitha."

"Well, Tabitha, if we can get you assigned, you'll be able to join the fight with the rest of us. But before any of that, you'll have plenty of time to rest."

"Okay. Thank you for saving us." I can see brokenness in her eyes, and I am overwhelmed with a desire to comfort her. When Zypher leaves, I work up the courage to talk to her.

"My name's Lucien."

"Hi." She keeps her head down, so I take that, along with the one-word answer, as a sign to leave her be.

I continue to walk next to her in awkward silence, hoping she'll eventually want to talk to me, but I am also content just to make her feel safe with my presence. She finally breaks the silence. "How long have you been fighting?"

"Many years, but today was my first fourth-dimension fight. I'm glad to have made it out alive."

"The other glowing men say you fought well."

I am surprised to hear this. "Well, I had to help."

"Do you have a family, Lucien?"

"No, they've all been killed by the fallen, but at least I know I'll see them again."

"Yes, you will. We can consider all the saved who have died to be blessed."

Now she's the one comforting me. Who is this girl? I try to maintain my masculine role. "I'm sure we'll be able to find your family."

Now I'm lying just to sound supportive.

"I hope so, but if they've passed on, at least I'll know they're with Him." She looks into my eyes for the first time when she says this, but only for a moment. She quickly puts her head back down. For that brief moment, when our eyes connected, I felt joy in the center of my chest. As we continue to talk, I long for more of that joy, and so I seek to look into her deep blue eyes again, but she isn't having it.

"So, what did you do back in Idaho?" I persist.

"I was a student. I was going to school for psychology on a soccer scholarship."

"Oh, wow—impressive. So are you psychoanalyzing me right now?" I jest.

She laughs. "No, I don't have the energy for that."

I hear Tyrus shout from the rear of the formation, "Stop hitting on the hostages, Lucien!"

The squad laughs. I laugh with them, but I am a little embarrassed as well. This poor girl has been through so much. The last thing she needs is some guy hitting on her right after she is rescued. But her reaction to Tyrus's comment is a giggle, so I guess that's a good sign. I try to back off, but I still find myself very intrigued with her.

"Well, you're safe now."

Obviously.

"I know. Thank you."

Now I'm just overstating the obvious. I'm starting to remember why I'm single.

"You all seem so kind. I don't understand."

"What do you mean?" I'm complimented yet confused.

"Well, you don't seem like the type of men who could kill, yet you killed all of those men so easily today."

"I think we had to."

"I wish I had the will to kill like you do."

No, you don't, I'm thinking.

"We do what needs to be done, but the weight of death is upon us nonetheless."

Am I just trying to sound deep now? I should stop talking.

"Whoa, pretty heavy-handed, don't you think?" she jokes.

"Ha ha … yeah … sorry."

We talk for the next few hours of the walk. I learn all about how her mother is sick with cancer, how no amount of prayer has cured her, and how it's tested her faith. She tells me about how this led to her wanting to learn how to comfort the dying, which led her into psychology.

Even though she's drugged and exhausted, she never falls out of formation. Most of the unassigned do fall out and need help, but not Tabitha. As I listen to her more and more, I take in her beauty. Her long, dirty blond hair blows in her face as she looks up at me, but she moves it aside, exposing her blue-green eyes. Her eyes give me that same warm, joyous feeling every time she lets me look into them. She's very petite and feminine, yet she moves like an athlete, effortlessly and gracefully. Everything about her is beautiful to me. I'd almost forgotten what it felt like to be infatuated, but I know now is probably not the best time for this. But on the other hand, with everything that's going on around us, is there a best time? I suppose not. I find myself praying in my mind while talking to her. I'm asking God to prevent me from making all the mistakes that I've made in the past with women—being too forward, too hasty, or too selfish, mistaking signals … Why am I even praying about this? What am I, dating this girl? I just met her and she's normal, and I'm glowing orange because I'm connected to an angel. What am I thinking? *Stop thinking and just enjoy this time. You'll probably never see her again anyway.*

Even though we just met, I feel like I've made a friend. I hope this isn't the last time I see her. I look up to the front of our formation and notice Zypher eyeballing me pretty closely. He motions for me to come up to him. I run up there, and I already have an idea of what he's going to say. "Do you realize we're still on a mission?"

He's pretty stern.

"Yes, I do."

"Then act like it. Look, I know she's hot. I'm a man too, but you can't think with your balls during a mission. Clear?"

"Roger, understood." I fall back in formation and avoid Tabitha. A couple of times I look back and see her looking at me as though she has more to say, but I resist and break eye contact. I'm hoping she's smart enough to understand that I just got my ass chewed. The rest of our journey back to the base under the mountain is spent helping the unassigned keep up. Sometimes we carry them, sometimes we have to stop, but we eventually make it with everyone intact.

When we arrive, we immediately hand the hostages over to a medical team to be treated. Most of them are just traumatized and dehydrated. Although it pains me to know what they've been through, I rest in the fact that we have ended their suffering, at least for now.

I can't sleep that night and decide to spend some time in one of the common areas. The common areas are not what you would expect to see on a military base. It's clear that a great deal of effort was put into making them places of peace. I suppose the times call for it. Each area has several comfortable couches, all facing a fireplace. The couches are all set in a semicircle, like theater seats with the fireplace being a thrust stage. All the people sitting on the couches can see each other and converse. The walls are the same green stone, which I have found out is jade. The fireplace is made of black volcanic rock. It almost looks like marble. The floor is a soft dark blue carpet that makes you want to take your boots off so your toes can feel its softness.

When I arrive in the area, I see that although we have given the rescued hostages their own rooms, they would much rather be together. I'm guessing they're also having trouble sleeping. When I enter, they're all holding hands while an elderly man prays. I stand silently and listen. His prayer is very heartfelt, and it touches me. It's full of thanksgiving and praise to the Father for what He's done for them. He prays that they can still be used for God's kingdom. He prays for the dead. He prays for those of us who freed them and brought them here. He even prays for the fallen. When he finishes, they all open their eyes and notice that I'm standing there. I'm welcomed with smiles.

"Hello, Lucien," the old man says. I'm surprised that he knows my name and embarrassed that I don't know his. "Hello, sir. I apologize, but I forgot your name."

"It's okay, son. I never told it to you. It's John. Have a seat. Join us."

"Thank you, sir."

It's a very welcoming environment. When I sit down, they all look at me as though I am about to tell a story.

"So, Lucien, how long have you been fighting alongside these boys?" John talks to me like a son.

"This was actually my first mission."

"Really? Well, we can't express in words how grateful we are for what you boys did for us."

"Thank you for saying so, sir."

"John. Please."

I look around the room and notice Tabitha seated on one of the far left couches. She gives me a look that says, *Hi! About time you noticed me.*

I can feel my heart rate rapidly increase with excitement. I see John notice me looking at her. He just smiles to himself. I'm looking around at these people, and I am amazed by how at peace they look. I would have expected them to be full of fear and scared of their own shadows after the ordeal they just went through. But they are all leaning on one another, allowing God's peace to let them be in this moment and nowhere else.

"How did you all maintain while you were captured?" I ask John.

"Can I tell you a story, Lucien?"

"Sure."

"When I was about six, my father took me on a white-water rafting trip. This was before the war started, mind you. The beast hadn't even come to power yet. Anyway, I had heard of white-water rafting, and being an ignorant six-year-old, I thought it sounded like fun. But I had no idea what I was in for."

Everyone in the room is giving John their full attention. I get the sense that he is respected by the group not only as a wise elder, but also as a storyteller.

"So, we get into the raft, and I'm ecstatic, right? The raft has about six people in it, but I'm the only child. Now, as we start down the river, I'm having fun at first. But then it starts to get a little bumpy. I look to my father to see if this is normal, and he gives me a comforting nod. Then the white water comes. When we hit it, we're thrown left and right. "Daddy!" I yell, clamping the side of the raft for dear life. At this point I really believe I'm going to be thrown from the raft. My father gently puts his hand on my shoulder and looks me in the eye. "You're okay, son. I've got you." He holds me close to him, and from then on through the rest of the trip, I feel like no amount of white water could pry me from the grip of my father's powerful arms. I spend the rest of the trip laughing every time we hit turbulence. It was a blast."

He pauses in thought for a few serious moments.

"Now, don't get me wrong, Lucien. I'm not saying that what we just went through was fun. But our heavenly Father's arms were around us the whole time. And even those of us who didn't finish the trip are now in His arms forever."

I see tears forming in the eyes of many of the listeners. A long silence follows. I can feel the gratefulness in the room. It's like we're all thankful together as one person. I feel blessed for having the privilege of being used as the Father's instrument. One by one the people go off to their rooms, finally able to accept the comfort of safety and go to sleep. I'm hoping that somehow I'll be left alone with Tabitha so we can talk. But she tells me good night and leaves. I'm left alone with John.

"So, Lucien, do you feel like telling me what's troubling you?"

That was blunt.

"What do you mean, John?"

"You may have the glow of an angel, but I see pain in your eyes. It's okay if you'd rather not talk about it, but can I at least pray for you?"

"Okay."

I'm wondering what it is he sees, but I hope he doesn't see my true pain. He sits beside me on my couch and places his hand on my shoulder.

"Heavenly Father, I can feel this man's pain. Oh, I see the

great things that you want to do through him, but I also see his burden. Lord, his heart is condemning him for past sins. Please, Lord Jesus, take his burden, and help him accept your grace and forgiveness."

I can't hide the tears that are falling on the floor as I weep. The familiar jerking of my abdomen as I try to hold back the sounds of my crying is seizing me. It's usually very humiliating to cry in front of a stranger, but there's something about John's presence that makes me feel safe in doing so. I suppose that's why I'm crying so hard. He continues to pray as I cry. "Lord, please strengthen this man in the power of your name and affirm to him that he is forgiven and is your child. Please remind him, Father, that nothing in this world or in the next could ever change that. I pray all of this in Jesus's precious name. Amen."

As I continue to weep, I feel like a healing solution is being poured over the anguish in my heart. Can I truly be forgiven? Can God really remove this thorn from within me? I'm ashamed to even be asking these questions, because I know I'm supposed to believe in His grace and forgiveness. But something reminds me in that moment that before everything, what God wants is an honest heart.

"I so want to believe I can be forgiven."

Now I'm thinking out loud. "I believe in His power, but I have so much trouble believing I'm worthy of His grace."

John looks at me and slowly raises his brow.

"Let me save you that trouble, Lucien, and tell you that you're not worthy. None of us is. That's why it's a gift that all we have to do is accept. Can you just accept it?"

"I think so."

"Let go of the feeling you have to punish yourself. Jesus already took the punishment. It's done."

These words hit me hard, and I start crying again. I bow my head in prayer and am overflowing with thankfulness.

"Thank you, Lord. Thank you. Thank you. Thank you."

Like a cool breeze, freedom invigorates me. I am renewed in a way I am sure I have never felt. "Thank you" is all I can say, and I just keep saying it. When I'm finally done, I look up at John and suddenly realize how strong he is. He's the one who's been through the real ordeal, and here he is taking on my burdens. I wipe my tears and stand, offering him my hand.

"Thank you so much, John."

He takes my hand and then pulls me in to an embrace. "You're gonna be all right, son. Just let go and trust in Him." He pulls away and sighs. "As for me, I'm gonna go get some sleep. G'night."

He leaves me with that, and I remain staring at the fire. I feel fully at peace. I know I've repented of my sins, but I don't think I've truly let my grip off them, and the guilt that comes with them, until now. This feeling must be the "peace that surpasses all understanding" that Paul was talking about. I fall into a deep sleep right there on the couch.

CHAPTER

RESUSCITATION

his slumber is the deepest and most peaceful sleep I think I've ever known. My dreams are timeless and beautiful. I can't quite focus on the reality or substance of them, but at some point I find myself in the forest again, walking with Octavian. In his hand is a small package of salami. Casually, he takes pieces out of the package and eats them as we walk.

"So it looks like you're finally starting to understand what His sacrifice was all about. That's great. Not only will that give you some peace, but it'll make us stronger in battle. So what's up with the Tabitha girl? You like her?"

"I guess." He already knows what I'm thinking.

"You 'guess'? No, I think you like her. And hey, I don't blame you. Who wouldn't? She's got the kind of beauty that many of us came down to Earth for so long ago."

"So that really happened?"

"Oh, yeah. I didn't come down though. I tried to warn my buddies, but they wouldn't listen. It pissed off the Father something awful. He didn't banish them or anything, but He took their women from them, and He let them live with the pain of lost love for a couple centuries. I was glad I stayed up there. Anyway, take it slow with this girl. She's been through a lot. Plus, she's destined to be a pretty powerful warrior."

"What? But she's a woman."

"And? You think you men having more physical strength makes you spiritually stronger as well? You may be the ones the Father charged with leading, but you haven't seen a woman fight in the fourth dimension yet. Just wait."

"Wow, I had no idea."

"And you still don't. But do take peace in the fact that any time you do spend with Tabitha is a gift from the Father. Enjoy and cherish it."

"Okay, I will." I redirect the conversation. "Are we fighting again soon?"

"I don't know. Do I look like a prophet to you? I'm sure we'll fight again, but only God knows when. Why He won't tell us all the time is a mystery even to me. You know, I've been in some nice dream forests, but this one is exceptional. I don't recognize it as being on Earth. Did you get it from a movie or something?"

"No, just the gift of imagination, I suppose."

"Well, I like it. Let's meet here more often." He smiles at me. "All right, I'd love to stay here and hang out, but it's time for you to wake up. Somebody's bringing you coffee."

I'm slipping out of my dream into consciousness, but my eyes are so heavy that I simply can't open them. I feel someone's presence near me, so I know I have to wake up. I take a running start, so to speak, in trying to jerk my eyelids open a few times. They finally start to crack open. I have a feeling of peace and new life within me that I've never woken up with before. As my vision comes back, I look around, and I am pleased to see Tabitha sitting on the couch next to me. My heartbeat quickens. I was sure I couldn't be any happier. It is nice to be wrong.

"Good morning," she says in that sweet voice that makes me smile. "I brought you some coffee."

She gestures to the coffee table in the center of the room, where a steaming white porcelain cup is sitting.

"Oh, thank you so much." I take it and sit back, sipping it in total enjoyment.

"Did you sleep well?" I ask her.

"Definitely ... first full night's sleep I've gotten in a long time. How about you?"

"Oh, yeah."

"How did your talk with John go?"

"It was ... healing."

"Yeah, he's got a way of leading people to truth. So, I've never actually seen a person who's been assigned an angel before you guys came to get us. I've heard the stories but didn't know for sure until now that you guys actually glow."

"Yeah, it's a cool side effect. We don't even need flashlights in the dark."

She giggles like a chipmunk. Yes! I made her laugh again.

"Thanks so much for the coffee."

"You already said that, dork."

I smile. Our familiarity feels very warm.

"So, did they tell you if and when you'll be assigned?"

"No, I think they're just giving us all time to recover. Plus they're looking for our families so we can be reunited with them."

I almost forgot about that. "Did they find out anything about your family yet?"

"No."

"I'm sorry."

"It's okay. I'm learning in these times how to make the people I'm with my family." She looks me deep in the eyes when she says this. I look back and savor her trusting me enough to give me her eyes.

"I'm learning the same thing." *Please keep looking at me.*

"Where's your family?"

I'd rather not get into that, but I answer, "They were executed when the worship laws were put in place."

"Oh. I'm so sorry. Did you have kids?"

"Nope. Never been married either. The whole war thing's been taking all my time." I return my gaze to her and smirk.

She receives me warmly. "Well, I believe God will make time for what matters. I mean, look at us. There's a war going on, but we have time to sit and drink coffee by a fireplace."

She has a point.

"I suppose you're right. So why did your parents name you Tabitha?"

"Because I was pronounced dead at birth, but I was resuscitated by a nurse who just wouldn't accept my death."

I'm remembering what Octavian told me about her.

"God must have a plan for you."

"I'm sure he does. Just wish I knew what it was!" She laughs while masking some frustration.

"I have a feeling you're going to find out soon."

"I hope so."

We share some more comfortable silence before Tyrus enters. "Hey, guys. Tabitha."

He gives me a look that says, *You sly dog.* Then he sits down, holding his own cup of coffee and enjoying the fire. I find myself sitting up now, awaiting orders. He looks at me, and he motions for me to sit back.

"Relax, bro. I'm not here to take you anywhere. Zypher's giving us a couple days off, since it was a tough mission."

Those words melt like butter on my ears. "Seriously?"

"Yeah. Enjoy it, my friend."

If I had my way, I would sit in front of this fire with Tabitha the whole time. Just as the thought enters my mind, she gets up and leaves.

"Bye, Lucien. Tyrus." She gives him a deep voice that mocks how he greeted her. I watch her leave, and she looks back at me, catching me. We are both smiling, embarrassed in that moment, looking away from each other.

"Tyrus, dude, thanks a lot."

"What? Like I made her leave? She probably had to pee or something."

We share a chuckle.

"So, I saw some of what you did yesterday. Are you sure you don't have 4D training?"

"Only from you."

He smiles and swells with pride a bit. "Well, I suppose I am a pretty good trainer. Ha. But yeah. Good stuff, bro. Even Zypher was talking about you a little."

A little's good enough for me.

Something I don't quite understand has been on my mind. Since we've finally stopped for a while, I find my thoughts have time to get organized and be reflected upon. "Tyrus, I don't understand what the difference is between what we were fighting yesterday versus what you all fought on the first day we met."

"Oh, yeah. That was confusing for me too. The fallen can accompany an assigned person, or they can freely move about without a person. The advantages they have while being assigned is that they're a little stronger and they can fight in the third and fourth dimensions."

"So if they're weaker alone, how did the two men get killed in that first battle?"

"Well, that was because there were so many of them. When they travel without assigned people, they travel in much larger groups, so it's easier for them to blindside us. If we come across a pack like that again, you have to be most careful about watching your flanks. That's how they kill us."

It hits me how much more I have to learn about 4D warfare, and how lucky I am to have made it out alive yesterday.

"But, hey, we're on liberty, so let's not talk about work." He adds a log to the fire and sits back down. "I wanna hear more about this Tabitha girl."

I squirm in my chair a little bit.

"Bro, a lot of us tried to talk to her, but she wouldn't respond."

"I don't know what makes me so special." I feel like a king inside.

"We all figured she was just too traumatized. But she responded to *you* for some reason. Think she likes you, or what?"

"Oh, I don't know. It's nice just to talk to a woman again after being around all you smelly dudes for so long."

"I hear that." He laughs.

"So what do you guys usually do on liberty?" I shift topics.

"Mostly just hang out like this. We like to play poker sometimes … drink a little wine. We're doing that tonight if you wanna join us. But I totally get it if you need a break from the same personalities."

"Let me think about it." But I know I'd rather run into Tabitha again.

"Yeah, I know what you're thinking about." He winks at me, pats my knee, and then gets up to leave.

"Anyway, bro, just wanted to tell you we had libo. Poker's in my room tonight if you wanna go."

"Thanks, Tyrus."

He leaves. Once again I'm left in front of the fire, alone with my thoughts. It's still actually really nice. I start thinking about the man I killed on the mission. I play the incident over and over again in my head, and I wonder if I could have defeated him without killing him. This circumstance leads me to ask myself, and then God, if there is any hope for the fallen people. And if so, is there any hope for the fallen angels? And if there is, could angels still rebel? And if so, could I still rebel when I'm in heaven?

These thoughts are driving me crazy because I know these questions won't be answered this side of heaven. And I suppose I already have some of the answers to these questions, but I don't like them. So I keep asking the same questions, hoping to deduce different answers. I'm just glad that some things are beyond my understanding. I don't think the human heart has the capacity to take the pain that comes along with the true, intimate knowledge of some horrific truths.

It makes me wonder what kind of capacity the Father must have for pain, as He loves all and also knows all. Maybe that's why he allows us to fall in love with one another. It's a welcome antidote to much of the pain that inevitably comes with this life. Or perhaps it's just a preview of His true love for us. Either way, I welcome it in this lifeless land, where war and death seem to rule all of our daily motivations.

Zypher comes into the room and looks at me like he's been looking for me. I quickly stand, ready to receive orders.

"Hey, Lucien, are you coming to the morning service?"

"I didn't even know there was one."

"Oh, yeah. There's one every morning."

I probably have morning breath and need a shower, but I guess I'll have to deal with it.

"Come on. It's starting."

I follow him through some of the green hallways to a large gathering room where people are singing praise music to God. There's a big stage on which a band is playing and singing. There are three lead singers in front of the group lined up behind three microphone stands. A man with white hair and a small tuft of silver facial hair below his lip stands in the middle. On his right flank is a beautiful young woman singing upper harmony and playing an acoustic guitar. To his left is a tall, lanky man with dark-framed glasses singing lower harmony. Behind the singers is a beautiful set of pipes and an organ, as well as an electric keyboard, a set of drums, a bass guitar, and a cellist. Their voices and instruments fill the room and resonate deep in my chest. I feel tethered to my almighty God. The ceilings are very high and are lined with beams of dark, shiny wood. The people are clapping and moving, standing in front of red cushioned chairs. I follow Zypher to where the squad is standing. They've saved a seat for me.

"Why didn't Tyrus tell me about this?" I ask Zypher.

"Don't mind him. He's a bit scatterbrained sometimes."

I look down our row and see Tyrus, who gives me a thumbs-up, probably not even remembering that he didn't tell me about the service. I join in the worship music, which feels so healing and refreshing. As I'm singing, I notice a large sign on the wall that looks like it's been hand-woven. It reads, "Lord, make me a servant." It hits me that everything I'm doing should be in joyful service, not fearful duty as it has been. He's with me, and He is making me more like Him.

After the worship, an older assigned man comes out and gives an awesome sermon on how to find love in the midst of pain and chaos. I feel like the sermon is just for me, and I'm hoping Tabitha is here to hear it as well. But then I think, given the climate, that I'm sure the message speaks to just about everyone in the room.

The service closes with some more awesome worship. I go back to my room, clean up, and then head back to the common area, hoping to run into Tabitha again. I stare at the fire and relax for about an hour before Tyrus comes in. "Hey, bro."

He seems a little somber.

"Hey. You good?"

"Yeah, I'm good. Just got some bad news for you, bro. Well, it's good news, but it's bad news for you."

"What?"

My first thought is I'm being moved a different squad, an idea I hate.

"Well, they found Tabitha's family. They've been hiding out in

Idaho. So they immediately arranged transport for her, and she headed out. Sorry, man."

My heart sinks. Every shred of hope and love that had been growing in me as I thought about that incredible girl has just been dashed to pieces. I'll never see her again.

"Well, is she coming back?"

"I don't see why she would, bro. If you had a family in a place like Idaho, would you want to come back to the scorched third?"

"I guess not."

Talk about something ruining your day. He pats me on the back.

"It's all right. She's not the last woman on Earth."

Yeah, but for the short time I've known her, she's been the only woman on Earth to me. Regardless, I try to play it off.

"I'll be good. Thanks, man."

He nods solemnly and leaves me alone.

My mind races. *Why do I ever allow my hopes to get up in the first place? It's almost easier to just not hope at all. Okay, stop it. This is a very familiar train of thought. Don't fall into its trap again. You know it only leads to bitterness and despair, and that helps nothing. Just be thankful that you got to meet such an amazing girl and that you got to spend some time with her. Yeah ... easier said than done. This sucks.*

I spend the rest of that night sulking in my room. I feel like a brokenhearted twelve-year-old. Maybe it's just been so long since I've had any romantic involvement that the callous on my heart fell off, making me vulnerable once again to puppy-love heartache. I feel ridiculous. I'm supposed to be a warrior. What the hell is wrong with me?

I need to go find something to get my mind off this. I wonder if there is a gym here. I go walking around the halls, asking people if there is one. A very large unassigned man in a chef's outfit jovially points me in the right direction.

It takes me a while to find the place. The hallways are like a maze. It's amazing to me how narrow the hallways are, and yet so many rooms are so large and elaborate. I open the door to the gym, and I am surprised by the size of it. It's about the size of a football field, filled with weights and machines. I know that being assigned has made me stronger, but I'm curious how much stronger. So, like any vainly prideful man, I start with the bench press. The most I was ever able to do when I was unassigned was 315 pounds, so I start with that. It feels like I'm just warming up. I easily do twenty reps and put it back. I add 100 pounds. My muscles are barely warm. I keep adding 100 pounds until I get to 915 pounds … finally a bit of a challenge. I'm able to do fifteen reps. At 1,015 pounds, I'm able to do ten reps. I bring the weight up to 1,215 pounds, and I am able to do six reps. I decide to stop there. I'm having trouble believing these weights weigh what they say they weigh, but I look around the room and see a very large unassigned man who looks like a bodybuilder having trouble bench-pressing 450 pounds. The numbers are correct. My strength is real.

Just for kicks, I try a barbell deadlift. I can do six reps at 2,000 pounds. The metal on the barbells is thicker than what I've seen. Clearly they've been adapted to handle the heavy weight.

In the next room, there is a track. I used to play football, so I'm wondering what my forty-yard dash time is. My personal best time was 4.8 seconds. A lanky man is running laps past me. I see he is wearing a wristwatch. My eyes catch his, so I stop him to ask if he can time me.

"Why, so you can show off?" He rolls his eyes at me, sweat glistening on his forehead.

"Nah, man. It's all new to me. I'm just curious," I say as humbly as possible. I think not being assigned yet has made him a little bitter. He gives in and nods his head. I get into a three-point stance, beaming with anticipation. I take off, launching forward and surprising myself as I barely feel my feet touching the ground. The air against my face feels like my head is outside a car window on the freeway. Passing the forty-yard mark, I slow down, stop, and turn around. The lanky man holds up his watch with an indifferent look on his face. "3.1 seconds," he says, as though tired of saying it. Oh, if I could play football now. But I suppose the playing field would be equal if it were against all assigned men. Regardless, it is all pretty cool. And it's getting my mind off Tabitha. *Oh, I shouldn't have thought about her.* I feel a surge of heartache. It's taken away my desire to eat, but I know I should.

I see some of the squad in the cafeteria, but I decide to eat alone. I can barely eat half of my food. I go back to my room and try to take a nap. Unable to fall asleep, I just pray and try to give my burden to God. A peace comes over me, and I fall asleep.

When I wake up initially, I feel normal. Taking a deep breath, I observe my surroundings. Then Tabitha's blue-green eyes flash through my mind. The pain in my chest and stomach returns. I wish I had some way to contact her. I know I'm gonna have to do something to distract my mind again. What about Tyrus's poker game? I check the time and see that it's about eight at night. I might as well head to his room and check it out. I don't have anything else productive to do.

I knock on his door, and he answers with a cigar in his mouth and a smile on his face. "What's up, dickweed?"

He puts his arm around my shoulder and drags me in. I can tell he's had a few drinks. The rest of the squad is there, minus Zypher. Spero hands me a cup of wine and gives me a little noogie. They're all sitting around a cliché poker table, drinking wine from brown porcelain cups, smoking and dipping tobacco. There's an open seat next to Apollo, and he waves me over to sit by him. I can see that he still doesn't have his glow back. His angel must still be recovering. His gesture for me to sit near him surprises me. Up to this point, I thought he didn't like me. I sit down next to him.

"Don't think just 'cause I'm temporarily unassigned means I won't still kick your ass."

He jests, giving me a little chin-check punch. This is the first time he's joked around with me. It makes me feel welcomed.

There's a looming cloud of smoke in the room that I initially thought would bother me, but now that I'm getting to inhale some of it, I find that I enjoy it.

"Can I get a cigarette from somebody?" I ask.

Apollo hands me one and lights it for me. Inhaling the smoke is like sweet nectar to my body. I can't remember the last time I smoked, but I can tell that I've missed it. Why it feels so good to abuse your own body, I'll never know.

"What are we playing?" I ask Apollo.

"Texas hold 'em. You know how to play?"

I know that I do, but I can't remember learning it. I suppose some of my memories still remain lost.

"Sure, what are we going to play with?"

It occurs to me for the first time that I haven't seen any currency used anywhere in this place.

"Well, we all start with a thousand in chips, and it's no limit hold 'em 'til there's only one man left." The cards clap together as he shuffles them.

"And what does he win?" The stakes seem to matter to me.

He eyeballs me. "All the losers have to clean Tyrus's room."

"Hilarious. Awesome."

This should be fun.

Although I remember how to play poker, I also remember very quickly that I'm not very good at it. Within an hour, I'm down five hundred chips. It looks like I'm gonna be doing some cleaning.

After a few cups of wine, I start to open up a little and join the conversation. The guys are all talking about women, of course, so naturally everyone's an expert. I open my big trap and add my advice to the situation. "The thing with women is they just want to be controlled. They're like a bunch of lost puppies that need to be rescued and trained."

I can taste the foolishness of my words as they leave my lips. I know I want to lead, but I think I took it too far just to sound tough. The guys see right through me.

"Oh, really? Okay, General Patton, so explain to all of us how you took control with Tabitha." Zuriel's got my number.

"Ooohhh snap!" Apollo chimes in.

I try to save face.

"I was just biding my time—that's all, being patient," I say with a sheepish smile while taking the last thing I need: another gulp of wine.

"Oh, is that what you were doing? Well, looks like your plan bit you in the ass, 'cause now she's gone, dingleweed."

I know Zuriel's just poking fun, but the truth of his statement stings a bit. I just smile and try to play it off. Tyrus clears his throat, preparing to speak, and everyone goes silent. "Gents, here's the thing with women."

The men's respect for him is demonstrated by their giving him their full attention.

"We all know what God has to say about it: 'Love her like Christ loved the church,' yes?"

We all nod as if we understand fully what that means.

"Well, how did he love us?" He waits for an answer but gets none.

"He died for us. When you meet a woman who you know in the bottom of your heart you would die for, then you'll know what it means to love a woman. And she'll respond to that love in kind because it's pure and true."

We are all silenced by this powerful truth. It's the kind of thing that your heart knows is true, but to hear it makes you uncomfortable because you know you fall short of it.

Tyrus chuckles. "Don't look so down, fellas. Denying yourself is a good thing, and you all know it."

Just then he flips over his cards, revealing a full house, aces over kings, and we remember that we were on the last round of a hand.

"Booya!" he shouts in victory, raking in the large pot of chips.

"Well, Apollo, looks like it's just you and me, junior."

Tyrus gives him a half-cocked smile. Apollo slouches in his chair, like this isn't the first time Tyrus has given him a beating in poker. He leans over to me. "He always wins. I swear, he just has these poker nights when he needs his room cleaned."

A few more hands, and Tyrus cleans out Apollo, doing a signature victory stretch that I've seen him do at the end of battles. His arms high overhead and with a deep sigh he says, "All right, ladies, it's been a good night, but daddy's goin' to bed. You guys can clean tomorrow."

"Yeah, yeah," we all say sporadically.

I stumble my way back to my room, having not had any alcohol for an unknown eternity. My tolerance is shot. In bed, I try to pray, but the room is spinning and my thoughts are all over the place. But they always return to Tabitha. I wonder what she's doing right now, what she's thinking, if she's forgotten about me already. Was my connection with her just an illusion? Why would she leave without saying goodbye?

Just then there's a loud knock on my door. I sit up quickly, startled. *Was that real?* I wait a few seconds. Bang, bang, bang. *Okay, it's real.* I open the door, and it's Tyrus, smiling with an envelope in his hand. "Dude, I think she thought my room was your room."

I know exactly what he means, but I play dumb so he won't think my every waking thought is of her. "What? Who?"

"She left you a note, dumb ass! She slipped it under my door thinking she was giving it to you."

He hands me an envelope that says, 'Lucien,' on it. I want to tear it open the moment it touches my fingers, but I hide my enthusiasm until he leaves.

"Good night, douche," he says as he walks away. I close the

door and rip open the envelope. It reads, in perfect feminine handwriting,

> Hey, Dork,
>
> So I just found out where my family is, and they told me I'd have to leave right away if I want to see them. I couldn't find you, so I'm writing you this letter to say goodbye, or at 'least "see you later." I want to be assigned an angel and join the fight, so hopefully we'll run into each other again. Thanks for listening to me and being my friend. Oh, yeah, and for rescuing us from horrible captivity and all. LOL. I would have stayed, but I found out my mom's cancer came back, so I need to go be with her. Miss you already, dork,
>
> Tabitha

Wow. She said she missed me. I allow the horrible thought that her mom will probably pass soon to enter my mind, and I immediately feel guilty for thinking it. What is it about this girl? I don't care, I'm just going to pray every day that I get to see her again. It'll make this whole war a tolerable thing to live through. After reading her a note a couple more times, I fall asleep with it in my hand like a hopeless romantic.

CHAPTER

SITTING POST

When I wake up, I'm hungover, but the pain in my chest and stomach is gone. I look at the note again and smile.

Although I'm spinning and have a headache, I'm terribly hungry, probably from the workout. I move my arms and legs, and I feel the soreness setting in. I guess I'm not immortal, just stronger.

In the cafeteria I look for the squad. I find them, and they look like they've been waiting for me. I sit down and feel like I'm in trouble.

"Looks like you guys had fun last night, huh?" asks Zypher as he looks into my bloodshot eyes.

"It's all right. I told you guys to enjoy your time off. All right now, since you're all here, listen up."

I can tell this is serious.

"Starting tomorrow, we're on post."

"Post?"

"Post?"

A couple of the squad protest.

85

"That's right." Zypher looks at each of us as if to say, *I'd better not hear another word of bitching.* Everyone quiets down.

"After our mission the other day, we got word that it pissed off the fallen higher-ups something awful. We made them look bad to the world, and now they're looking to make an example of us. So the word is that they're planning an attack on this base. It's nothing new. I know we've been attacked before, but since they predict this one may be on a grander scale, they want elites on post. And here's the kicker: we're gonna be aboveground."

I don't totally understand, but the rest of the squad looks a little shocked. Come to think of it, I don't remember anyone challenging us aboveground when we entered the base, so I can only assume there isn't usually anyone on post aboveground. I ask the obvious question that should never be asked during any military operation: "Why?"

Now, I would usually expect an ass-chewing for a question like that, but in this case it seems warranted, since the whole squad looks at Zypher as soon as I ask it.

"It's just an extra line of security. They want the first line of defense pushed out farther, and we should take it as a sign that we're doing a good job, since they chose us."

The squad seems satisfied with that answer, but personally I'm not crazy about the idea of sitting aboveground, exposed and waiting to be attacked by God knows how many fallen.

"Of course, we'll have comm with the inside, and four elite squads will be on QRF round the clock."

QRF is "quick reaction force" in civilian terms.

"The watch is gonna go in twenty-four-hour shifts for a week, so we'll be twenty-four on, twenty-four off, and then wait for further orders."

Zypher seems so unshaken. As I listen to him talk, I wonder how many battles he's been in. I'm sure it's more than I've seen, even in my new memory.

"All right, that about covers it. Meet in our common area

tomorrow at the fourth hour." He gets up and leaves like he's got to be somewhere. We're all left looking at each other as if to ask, *Are you ready for this?*

Tyrus is nodding his head with a joyful smile on his face. "All right, fellas, this could very well be seven days of staring at dust, but you all know that we're gonna have to be ready every second."

Then he loses his smile and stares at each of us intently. "And look, I know you're all above this, but if I catch any one of you sleeping, I swear I'll punch you in the face."

No one laughs, because we know he means it.

For the rest of the day, I lounge in our common area staring at the fire. So much has happened over the last few weeks. *Have I been with the squad for only a few weeks?* It feels like I've had a lifetime of experiences with them already. Although I feel regenerated from the time we've had off, and I feel energized from being assigned, my soul still feels weary from all the war I've seen, before and after I was captured. The thought that all of this will never end in my lifetime haunts me terribly, giving me a heaviness in my stomach that hurts on a deeper level than nausea. *When is He coming back? What is the point of all this fighting? He could end all of this in a second if He wanted to, so why doesn't He?* It makes no sense to me. My eyes are getting heavy as I stare at the beautiful flames in the fireplace. I don't fight it and let them close.

When I wake up, the fire is smoldering. I look at the clock on the wall and I see that it's 2 a.m., or the second hour. I have two hours to get ready. It's good that the cafeteria is open twenty-four hours.

I'm ready with my gear by halfway through the third hour. When I get back to the common room, the whole squad is already there, minus Zypher.

"Lucien, what's up, brotha?" Apollo greets me, and I see that he's been assigned again. I take a playful stab at him. "Looks like you've got that nice glow back. Now I can smack you around again."

"Like you could before," he bites back.

As I hang out with the squad, I'm trying to hide my pregame jitters. But I feel all right with it, because I sense that they have some of their own—except for Tyrus, who is jovial as always. Zypher shows up and gives us a quick briefing on our post positions. It will be two men per post, one sleeping, one awake, three hours up, three hours down, for twenty-four hours. He tells us it's time to go, and the men slowly start picking up their gear, taking their time.

"Hey, what did I just say? Move your asses!"

We all see that he's in no mood for apathy, and we hurry up and follow him. I walk next to Alcyone.

"What's up with Zypher?" I ask him.

"Oh, don't sweat it. He's like that when the higher-ups chew his ass."

The idea of Zypher getting chewed out by anyone seems unreal to me.

"What? What did he get chewed for?"

"Who knows? I know better than to ask."

We head up several staircases that wind like they're in an old church. Then we head up a few ladders that lead to another manhole cover with a combination lock on it. When Zypher opens it, a few gallons of dust fall on us in the tunnel. As soon as we surface, we sprint out to locations that Zypher briefed us on. We set up in a 360 that measures about five hundred yards in diameter, digging our fighting holes in pairs, with one man digging and one man keeping watch. I'm paired up with Spero, who keeps watch while I dig. Even with my new strength, it takes me about two hours to dig a four-foot-deep by four-by-six-foot-wide hole. The way the dust packs itself doesn't help. Just beneath the surface it's as hard as dry clay. I dig until my arms just won't dig anymore, but the hole is complete.

"Nice hole, junior," Spero tells me. "Go ahead and rack out. I'll take first watch."

He's already been lying in the dust on his stomach for two hours keeping a lookout. Now he climbs into the hole exposing just his head, and he gets ready to do it for three more hours. But I'm so exhausted from digging that I'm not going to argue with him, so I sit down in the corner of the hole while he stands and I fall asleep.

For the next twenty-four hours we switch positions back and forth every three hours. Zypher punches out with a team of four every few hours for a recon patrol.

At the end of our first twenty-four hours, we've seen only dust. We get relieved by another elite assigned squad, led by a towering man with an eye patch named Aeolus. As we're going back underground, he stops me. "So you're Lucien, huh?"

"Yes, sir."

He sizes me up with his one eye. "Bullshit. My name's Aeolus."

"Roger that."

"If Zypher will let you, you should train with us one of these days." He looks at me like he can't wait to break me.

"Roger that." I don't know what else to say.

"All right, enjoy your twenty-four hours off."

"Roger that."

Aeolus and Zypher talk for a bit as Zypher briefs him on the activity, or lack thereof.

We take twenty-four hours eating, sleeping, and relaxing belowground, and then we're back in our fighting holes. This rotation goes on for about five days, and we still haven't seen a thing.

On the night of the fifth day, it's my watch. I'm staring at the horizon through my binos. The sand is blowing across the ground, and at this point I've memorized the swirling patterns. However, this time at the base of the swirling clouds I see something new. My hands begin to tingle because the adrenaline has already surged through my body. It appears to be about two miles north on the flatland. I can't see a shape, just dust in the air as though something is running. I get on my radio. "Zulu actual, Lima 1!" I'm calling Zypher but suddenly realize that my excitement is causing me to yell into the radio.

"Send it," Zypher responds.

"I'm spotting movement about two miles to the north. How copy?"

"Roger, in route to your pos."

He's coming to me. Within thirty seconds he jumps next to me in my fighting hole with a pair of binoculars. He looks into the distance for a few seconds and then smiles.

"What?" I ask, relieved by his reaction.

The tension in his body releases, and he hands me the binoculars. "It's just a desert buffalo. They're a product of the scorching. How they survive in this environment is beyond me."

The binoculars on are on my face again. I'm eager to see this creature for myself. The buffalo is light brown and rail thin.

"Wow. Hilarious."

By now Spero's awake, and he takes a look too. "Oh, nice! Hey, skipper, can we kill it and bring it in?" He turns to me. "Those things make great burgers. We can give it to the cafeteria, and they'll prepare it for us."

Zypher thinks for a second. "I don't know …"

He looks again.

"I'm not sure why it's alone."

"Come on, chief. I'll go get it and bring it in."

"All right, but hurry up about it. And take Lucien with you. Double-time it. I'll sit your post til you get back."

"Ya-hoo!" yells Spero in celebration.

We head out, sliding down the mountain as if surfing. When we hit the flatland, we open up into a jog. Within six minutes we can see the buffalo. Spero fires a couple of shots midrun, and one round goes right through its skull, shooting blood out the back of its head.

"Nice shot," I say.

He goes to pick it up, and before I can blink he is overtaken by twenty or so faces made of black dust. His glowing white cloak flashes in the sea of darkness, but it's too late. I summon Octavian, but before he even appears, I see one of the faces enter through Spero's eyes and nose while his body freezes. Octavian is around me. Immediately, I charge one of the faces, colliding with it. The shriek pierces my ears. I remember what Tyrus said about watching my flanks. Quickly, I run backward and barely avoid a charging demon. Just as soon as I do that, I'm hit from the other side. This disorients me, but I'm able to counterattack, taking out another demon. I manage to dodge a few more shots and take out another demon.

A white light flashes by me. It's Zypher. He comes flying in, taking out two demons with one charge. I have no idea how he got here so fast. He must have had suspicions and followed close behind us. I'm hit from the side again, and this one does some real damage, separating me from Octavian and probably injuring him. I am now completely defenseless. I look up to see Zypher in action again. Anytime a demon comes near me, he takes it out; then without taking even a second to gain his bearings, he'll charge again to his flank, taking out the demon that's coming from the other side. I've never seen anyone else in the squad with his abilities and instincts. Within a minute or so he's taken out about ten of them, and the rest of them flee while they still can.

Once they've gone, I immediately hear horrifying screaming. Spero is holding his head and writhing in agony on the ground. Before we can even move, he points his wrist right at his own forehead and fires. His screaming stops, and his body goes limp. His bright red blood soaks into the dust, pouring out the back of his head. Black dust floats out of his eyes and mouth, and Zypher takes out the demon before it can flee. He quickly kneels down to

Spero's lifeless body and feels for a pulse. His face says it all. He gently picks up Spero's head and examines the back of it. I can see the pain in his eyes, but he exercises incredible emotional control.

It's hard for me to absorb what just happened, but I am in shock and mortified, not knowing what to say or do. Zypher looks me up and down to see if I'm seriously injured. Then he puts Spero on his shoulder and begins the walk back.

"Watch my six," he says, not even looking at me. On the way back we're met by a QRF squad led by Tyrus. Their angels are floating above them, ready for a fight. The men stop in their tracks when they see Zypher carrying Spero.

"Dead, or just out?" asks Tyrus.

"Dead. Demon-inflicted suicide."

Tyrus looks at the ground in silence.

When we get back to our posts, Zypher takes Spero's body belowground. He is gone for hours. We can all see that the guilt of Spero's death is heavy upon him. None of us blame him, but we all understand how he could blame himself.

The rest of the shift is done in silence. Zypher returns to take Spero's place in my fighting hole. Only a few hours ago, Spero was here with us. My stomach knots.

Aeolus's squad relieves us. They don't say much. We can see that they know what happened. They knew Spero as well.

The next twenty-four hours are kind of a blur. A vigil is held belowground in the small church after our shift. A few of the squad say some words about Spero and his bravery. They tell tales of his heroism in battle. I learn that his body is cremated. I am reassigned to Octavian within the day, which tells me he must not have been badly injured. The reassignment process is much like the assignment process, only not so formal. I am met by a different priest, who quickly reassigns me to Octavian through prayer. I imagine this is done with haste, as I am needed to return to my duties on the surface. The next day we go right back to our post. We've been given the obvious order from Zypher that all animals are off-limits from here on out. I find out from Tyrus that not even the higher-ups had ever heard of the fallen using a tactic like the buffalo before, which is probably why we fell for it.

The end of our week goes undisturbed, and we get the word that because of the attack, our post has been extended for a month.

We get word that Zypher has to go through a series of inquiries regarding Spero's death. We're all afraid that we might lose him as our squad leader. After a few days of investigation, Zypher is cleared, which we all find an incredible relief.

On our off time we don't see him at all. On our posts, he talks only business to us. Sometimes I'll see him staring off into the distance. I have many times been ashamed of the cowardly, selfish, insecure thoughts that run through my mind. I know for a fact that if I were in Zypher's shoes, I would be overwhelmed with shame and sorrow. When I look at Zypher lost in thought, it makes me wonder what his internal struggles are. Surely, a man as strong in mind and spirit as he doesn't share my insecurities. Or does he? He is, after all, human just like me. But he doesn't seem weak like me. What is the constitution of a man like that, and why can I never measure up? These are the things that torment me.

I've heard many people talking about great men getting their strength from the Lord. Although I know He is my savior, I don't know how to do that. I pray for it, yet I am still my same weak self. I have had intense experiences that should strengthen a man, yet my insecurities remain. Paul said that God gave him his thorn to keep him humble. Perhaps this is my thorn.

A couple of weeks go by, and we all start to fall into the monotonous routine of things. Our time on rest is quite enjoyable, but post is more and more miserable. Seasons in the scorched third overtake us with the relentless fury of extremes. When it's cold, it's well below freezing, and when it's hot, it surpasses 130 degrees Fahrenheit when the sun is at its hottest. Neither is tolerable. Moderate temperatures last a few mere days during seasonal transitions. Since we lost Spero, we've entered the cold season.

The only benefit to this desert is the lack of moisture. It almost never rains or snows, so we don't have to deal with the miserable combination of wet and cold. Just cold. But this cold is fierce. When I'm on post, even though I'm bundled up in four layers, my core feels like it's frozen. My skin isn't just cold, my bones are as well. It's a cold that goes so deep it takes hours belowground to feel circulation again. When I get into bed after a shift, I'm still shivering for an hour. I'm convinced that were it not for the strength I have from being assigned, I would have died from hypothermia by now.

After a few weeks (weeks that feel like months), our squad is finally granted a forty-eight-hour liberty. Aeolus's squad covers for us while we rest. Coffee is my companion. Morale is so low, we don't talk much to each other. Even though we are on liberty, we all carry radios as a precaution. My radio is on the table in front of me next to my warm coffee when suddenly a strange message crackles through it: "QRF up! QRF up!"

QRF has been called aboveground. That means that Aeolus's squad has been attacked, making us go from being on rest to now being the next QRF squad. We'll be called up if two squads aren't enough to handle the fight. I rush to my room and get my gear on, returning to the common area within five minutes. We haven't seen action since Spero was killed, so we're all a little eager to get up there. We listen to our radios, waiting for orders to come help. We all have been sitting in silence for a few minutes when we hear someone open the mic on the other end. Everyone stands, ready to move.

"QRF 2 aboveground. I say again, QRF 2 aboveground."

That's our cue.

We all sprint to the ladder tunnel, climbing faster than we ever have. As we're climbing, our white cloaks appear and surround us. Zypher opens the top manhole, and we see him float and charge the instant daylight appears. When I reach the surface, I am immediately immersed in chaos. There are shrieks, collisions, men yelling orders, and sounds of demon growls. I see several men laid out on the ground. Once our last man surfaces, about five men who are out run down the manhole, as they are now defenseless against these demons. I'm frantically looking around for something to charge when I am hit from the back. I fall to the ground, but my connection to Octavian remains intact. I jump in the air, do a 180, and take out the demon that hit me. I don't know how, but as soon as that collision is completed I sense something to my right and charge it, sending another demon into the abyss. I wonder in the moment if it at all resembled what I saw Zypher do on the flatland. The next few minutes are a blur as I take out a couple more demons and dodge some death blows. I see Zypher and Tyrus charge the same demon from different angles, smashing him into dust. It's the first time I've seen that tactic used. I didn't even know we could do it. Unfortunately, I see the fallen using the same tactic, and I actually witness them kill a man from Aeolus's squad.

I hit the ground in exhaustion after my last collision, unable to fight anymore. In the same moment, I see a demon charge me, and I wince in anticipation of my fate. Out of nowhere Aeolus comes spinning through the air like a corkscrew, destroying the demon and one I didn't see charging me from another angle. "I thought you were supposed to be tough." He looks at me with disappointment and shakes his head. I have nothing to say as I gasp for air, giving him a thank you salute.

The shrieks start to die down, and I can feel my heart pumping in my ears. I'm breathing as fast as is physiologically possible, yet I just can't get enough air. Men all around me are being carried belowground. I can't tell who is dead and who is alive. My vision is blurry, and I'm dizzy. After a couple of minutes hyperventilating and shaking, I find the strength to get up and help a limping man from another squad. He thanks me. I look down at his leg and see that it's bent sideways at the knee to a ninety-degree angle. The top of his head pours bright red blood that is going into his eyes. He doesn't even lift his hand to wipe it, so I take my medical kit off my hip and use a gauze pad from it to wipe his face. Then I press it into the wound on his head.

A third QRF squad suddenly shows up and takes post as the rest of us hobble belowground. I am relieved of helping the bleeding man, and I make my way down as well. It takes the last ounce of energy I own to find myself a hospital bed and lose consciousness.

The next few days consist of boring post, followed by memorial after memorial. Among three squads, six men were killed in the latest attack. None, however, were killed from our squad.

The next month is quiet aboveground. We all seem to agree that the enemy has launched its worst attack for the time being.

Another couple weeks go by, and the higher-ups retract the aboveground post, giving us some time off.

With this strange new freedom, my thoughts begin to turn to more pleasant distractions; namely, Tabitha. I thank God for leaving something beautiful behind in this scorched land, and I simultaneously resent Him for taking her away. My longing for connection to her consumes me to the point that I ask Zypher about writing to Tabitha. Without flinching, he tells me that all mail has been suspended for now, but that I can write anyway and mail the letters later.

I begin writing constantly. This conversation I begin to have through my letters to her, though one-sided, is therapeutic for me. Aside from prayer, thoughts of her have helped sustain me through the boredom and horror of the last couple months. I pour out my heart on the pages as I write her letter after letter. I tell her of my thoughts of her, how I miss her and hope to see her again, the terrible things I've seen, our successes in battle, and how it seems as though it will never end, and I write to her of faith in

Jesus. I hope she is maintaining her faith, and I am praying for her mother. I miss her smile, and I miss her laugh.

In the midst of writing, I start to question my motives for having affection toward her. Were I not in such circumstances, would I desire her company like I do, or am I just using her as an escape from the misery of the situation? I hope my love is genuine, and I pray that if it isn't, God will make it so. She is so precious to me, and she deserves true love.

We may have time off, but Zypher keeps us training. The first couple days we run the projectile course a few times as individuals, and then we run it as a squad. The squad run is interesting. It's a lot of fire and movement—moving while someone else is firing and vice versa. It's quite the art form. Although we do quite well, many of us still take a lot of hits from projectiles and have to go to the medical unit to recover.

After a few more weeks of training, we start to fall into a routine. The training is tough, but I'm quite comfortable with the routine: train, eat, drink wine and play cards, repeat. I like it. It's an escape from the horrors I've seen, and the horrors yet to come. And in my alone time, I continue writing to Tabitha, causing myself to fall even more deeply in love with her at the hand of my growing monologue. I'm clearly delusional.

CHAPTER

LIBO SECURED

 ne day Zypher calls a meeting after training. We are all expecting some kind of news, since it's a meeting at an unusual time. He tells us that we've got a mission in a few days. A few of the higher-ups are traveling on foot from our base to the base where I was originally brought for healing, and they need an escort. Because of our recent performances, we are selected. Since I've been on this base, I have met squads that go months without a mission. We always seem to get picked for the hardest missions. On one hand it's an honor, but on the other I would have hoped that good performance wouldn't be punished with heavy lifting. Oh, well. We have no choice but to suck it up and follow orders.

Zypher spends about a half hour briefing us on our route, possible threats, equipment needed, etc. Although I expect the mission to suck, part of me is just happy to go to the surface again. Living underground for too long can drive a man stir-crazy. Zypher tries to downplay it, but apparently the higher-ups that we're escorting were supposed to be at the briefing but didn't show. But what can we do? They severely outrank us.

The day of the mission, we finally get to meet the higher-ups that we're escorting. They are both assigned men that look to be in their forties. I can only guess how old they really are. Based on how young people look once they're assigned, I'd put them in their nineties. When they greet us, their greetings seem shallow. As a lower-ranking man, I've always resented this attitude from those in charge. It's like they are pretending to care who you are, but it's overtly obvious that they don't. Regardless, protecting them is our mission, and I have to see the value in their rank, even if I don't like them. After the initial shallow, less than genuine motivational speech one of them gives us, I try my best to avoid talking to them.

When we hit the surface, our two new additions fall right into formation with us. I notice that their noise discipline and patrolling techniques are actually quite flawless, although I shouldn't expect anything less from men of such experience.

When we stop to sleep, the two higher-ups separate themselves from us. Their *presence adds an uncomfortable level of tension to the squad. We all feel as though they're looking over our shoulders. Because of their status, neither one of them posts watch at night. But that's okay; I expected that. What gets on my nerves is when one of them keeps asking us for a pinch of dip tobacco. You'd think they would have access to their own supply. I try not to get too irritated and just keep reminding myself that the mission will be over soon.

I find it nice to be patrolling on the surface again. Even though this part of the Earth has been scorched by the Father's wrath, it gives me comfort to look in the distance and know His hand was upon it. When I scan the horizon, I realize that even with my newly improved vision, dust is still all I can see. I remember when I first woke to this, it filled me with fear and loneliness, but now it gives me peace. I think this is because it makes me feel closer to the Father. There's something about reaching my own limit of perception and knowing there is more beyond it that awakens a feeling of eternity in my heart. There is part of me that is eternal and experiences the joy of knowing that part is in the hands of the Father. I get glimpses of this peace that last only but a moment, but the little taste of it that I do get is sweeter than anything I've ever known. I believe it is a preview of what it's like to truly dwell in His presence. I suddenly wish Tabitha were here so I could share this feeling with her.

As I'm walking, staring off into the distance, and enjoying this moment, my peace is interrupted by movement in the dust about thirty yards to my left. I look closer, and it just looks like the dust is simmering or even boiling, if that were possible. I'm confused by what I'm seeing, so I tilt my head in curiosity, stupidly not saying anything to anyone. I creep closer to see what it is, and I am startled by Zypher's loud voice. "Lucien, look out!"

As soon as I look back at him in reaction to his warning, I'm blindsided. I don't even know what hit me, but it came from the ground, whatever it was.

"Ambush!" yells Zypher. Before I can get off the ground, I'm hit from above. This time I can see that it's a demon. It's hovering about six inches above my face, like a lion sniffing prey it's about to eat. I get a good look at this demon. It has a grotesque face like the face of a decomposing corpse. It smells like rotting flesh, and I can feel coldness, like I'm in front of an open freezer. There is fighting all around me, but I am paralyzed in horror by this demon.

Why I can't summon Octavian? Why is the demon not attacking me?

I quickly look at my hand, and it no longer glows. Octavian's been injured, and I am now defenseless against this evil being. And then it occurs to me: That's why it's hovering over me. It's enjoying my fear before it destroys me or enters my mind. I can only assume the rest of the squad is too busy to help me. I start to pray. My voice is frozen, so I start praying in my mind, begging God for help. No sooner does this prayer enter my mind, than a series of jackhammer-like collisions go off right in my face. The shrieks are horrible. I'm disoriented but also know that someone just saved my life. But the number of collisions makes me think that multiple people hit the demon all at once. I feel someone standing over me and look up to see who my rescuer is so I can give him a big hug. When my vision focuses, I recognize before me the most beautiful face I've ever seen. I know her, but she now glows. It's Tabitha. Overwhelming joy and confusion and love flood my soul.

"How did you—" Before I can finish the question, she charges to her right and I see her collide with a demon, again in the jackhammer-like fashion that she used to destroy the last demon. I start hearing these rapid-fire collisions all around me. I want to fight but remember my state of helplessness, so I just stay on the ground so as not to get in the way. In a flurry of black dust I see an entire squad of demons retreating in fear off into the distance. Standing amongst us now are beautiful, glowing women. Some of them bleed from cuts on their faces. All the men stand speechless, jaws on the ground. I'm not sure if their reactions are because a group of women just saved us, or if they're just mesmerized by their overwhelming beauty. Perhaps it's a combination of both. The only one of us not surprised is Zypher.

"I take it you gentlemen have never seen women in action before." He chuckles. "Thanks, ladies. That was definitely welcomed assistance."

"What's the matter? You need girls to fight your battles?" jests the tallest of the women. I take it she is their squad leader. She steps toward him with a snarky grin on her face.

"Well, sometimes it's nice to see you ladies get off your asses and do something."

They share what looks like a bit of a romantic gaze and then embrace.

"I missed you, Lethaea."

"I missed you too, cutie."

After a long hug, they look at each other and then separate, checking their respective squads. The vindictive side of me wants to see Zypher enamored with this woman so I'll have a bit of an "I told you so" for him, since he chewed me out for being distracted by Tabitha. On the other hand, who am I to tell him anything?

After Zypher checks me for serious injuries, I finally decide to get up and look for Tabitha. She's standing off to the side, waiting for me. Her hands grab one another, and she shifts nervously. She's never looked so feminine or so beautiful. Even in boots she looks cute. I walk toward her slowly, taking her in as I approach.

"Hey, you," she says with a growing smile.

"You ... you saved my life," I manage to squeak out. I can't believe she is within my reach.

"Well, you saved mine first. It only seemed fair." Her smile widens. I lunge forward and throw my arms around her. She wraps her arms around my neck.

I squeeze her like I'll never let her go. I realize as she squeezes back that because I'm separated from Octavian, she's much stronger than I am. I think she knows this and is relishing it a little. I stay in the embrace until I feel my windpipe starting to close.

"Okay, you can let go," I wheeze. She chuckles sheepishly.

"So you got assigned in Idaho?" I ask, rubbing my neck.

"Yeah, I wouldn't stop asking everyone I could, so they finally gave me some training and an angel. But I still don't know anything about 3D warfare. So you guys will have to handle that if it happens."

"Well, that's all I can handle at the moment." I gesture to my non-glowing body.

"Yeah, I noticed. Should I smack you around now while I still have the chance?" Her giggle falls out of her. My heart grows, and warmth spreads through me.

I half-smile. "I hope you're kidding." She giggles again and then gives me a kiss on the cheek. I swear that one little kiss takes away all of my pain. I'm standing there, floating on air when Zypher's booming voice shatters my peace. "Lucien, let's go! We gotta step it out. Ladies, if you please, fall in formation with us."

We get into a two-squad-sized *V* and begin patrolling in the direction of our destination, the healing base. I make sure I end up next to Tabitha. I don't want to ever be farther away from her than I have to be—not only because I want to talk to her, but also because if we're attacked again, I'd feel safe with her beside me. I don't care if Zypher chews me out.

"So how did you girls end up out here?" I'm eager to know how we got so lucky.

"They told us you were doing an escort to our base, and we got intel that ambushes were being set up on your route. So we came out to meet you and help you with any fighting." She pushes some loose hair behind her ear. "You guys were out of radio contact in the dead zone when we tried to get word to you, so we figured we'd just come out to you. It looks like we found you just in time too."

"Yeah, you did. Thank you again." I try not to stare too obviously at her delicate facial features.

"My pleasure. If I didn't, who would I have to bother by the fireplace?" She flashes her smile at me as we share fond memories. "So, how have you been?"

How have I been? I want to tell her I've missed her like a drowning man misses air. I want to tell her all I can think about are the sweet, unspeakably beautiful moments that we've shared. They are worth more than treasure to me, even as mere memories. All of this builds up beneath my vocal chords, but all that comes out is, "Good. I've been good. You?"

I'm realizing as she tells me all about her mother's death and her journey to the base where she was assigned that the reason I held back in telling her the true state of my heart is because I don't feel worthy of her love. My heart winces with expectation of the pain that will come when she rejects my love. I tell myself I am pitiful and stupid, but the insecurities remain.

I can feel her pain as she talks of mourning her mother, and even though I never met her mother, I feel like I'm mourning with her.

"I'm so sorry about your mom, Tabitha."

"It's okay." It's obvious she has worked through a lot of grieving. "Her suffering is over, and she's home now. I'm happy for her."

Her outlook on life and death is rooted in such certainty and faith. It must be this faith that gives her the peace she carries.

I look around and notice that I'm not the only one distracted by the beauty of the women. The single men among us are all engaged in conversation with women. Even Zypher is talking with Lethaea, but I see that even though he's talking with her, his eyes still scan the horizon. I snap out of my lovesick coma and start doing the same. The moment I begin doing this, impact rounds start cracking all around me.

"Contact left!" I yell, returning fire and diving to the ground. We fall right into our rhythm of fire and movement. The ladies' angels appear, encircling them in light. I can only fire shots, so I stay in the rear, watching the 4D action unfold.

It's over pretty quickly, and none of our people are hurt. Zypher has a fallen man pinned on the ground. He grabs him by his neck and stands him up, and then binds his hands with shackles that he takes out of his pack. The man no longer glows, so I know that his demon has been destroyed, but his eyes still shine black, indicating the enemy's ownership over him. As Zypher walks him into our formation, I can see the same indifferent look on his face that all fallen men have. It's like the fate of being captured was something he was expecting, and it has no effect on him. It's a somber demeanor but a consistent one nonetheless.

Aside from picking him up roughly, once Zypher sees full

surrender, he treats him like a human being. The rest of the men do as well. We all fall back into formation and continue patrolling.

The ambush has everyone alert, no longer happily conversing. We spend the rest of the trip that way and safely arrive at the healing base. As soon as we get there, the two higher-ups break away from us without so much as a thank you. We don't care; we're just glad they're out of our hair.

Zypher tells us we're off until the morning, and he escorts the prisoner out of our sight. I'm curious about his fate, but I'm ready to recuperate.

The rest of us go to the cafeteria, which is much nicer on this base than it is on ours. We enjoy the gourmet food and talk over our mission, making fun of the higher-ups. In the middle of our meal, Zypher walks up to our table. "What's up, fellas? Lucien, you're gonna have to cut dinner short. Come with me."

I want to ask why, but I resist the urge and just follow him. As we walk, he explains a little. "So, you remember the fallen man we just captured?"

"Yeah."

"Well, he says that he knows you and that if we want information, he'll only talk to you."

"Me? But I saw him. I didn't recognize him."

"Lucien, your memory has only begun to come back. You don't know what holes are still there. Either way, I want you to talk to him. Humor him with whatever game he wants to play, but be careful. He may know a lot about you. And the fallen are very deceptive, so try not to dwell on what he says. Just keep him talking and see if you can get any hard intel out of him."

"Roger that."

Even though I've defeated some of the fallen in battle, it still scares me to have to chat with one of them. They are ruled and motivated by pure evil. I'm clueless as to where to begin, but I can't let Zypher down.

We head much deeper into the base down staircases I've never seen before. Eventually, we end up in a hallway that looks like an old state prison with twenty-four-hour holding cells. Each one has a white metal door with a little window at head level big enough to see the prisoner's face, covered in thick glass. We stop at one of the cells. Zypher gives me a look of concern. "Here he is. I'm gonna leave you alone with him since he'll only talk to you, but I'll be in earshot if you need me."

He walks down the hall, leaving me at the door, which is all that separates me from this evil being. I step up to the glass and slowly peer in. I see him seated on the ground against the wall. He slowly looks up and notices me. His head is shaved, and he appears to be in his thirties. The arteries in his face and neck are black and brown. When he sees me there, a delighted smile grows on his face, as though a waiter has just brought him his food. We stare at each other in silence for about ten seconds.

"I'm sorry. Are you waiting for me to speak?" He enunciates like a Shakespearian actor.

"I thought you wanted to talk to me," I answer.

"Well, I do. Pardon my rudeness. My name is Agares. I realize you don't know me, but I know you, Lucien." The way he says my name sends chills up my spine.

"How do you know me?"

"Why, you're famous, of course. His majesty himself has a price on your head, but those in power convinced him to make you one of the forgotten when you were captured. Do you not remember this?"

"Some things are still a little fuzzy." I'm not sure what he's getting at.

"Ah, yes, the memory wipe. Well, for your benefit, may I fill you in?"

"Go ahead."

He pushes himself up and locks eyes with mine as he slowly walks to the glass. I back up a bit. His black eyes glisten.

"Well, first of all, it's an honor to meet you. Your passion in cruelty is legendary. You are responsible for more suffering than any of your counterparts, and for that I pay my respects."

I cringe inside, trying not to let him see I'm affected, but he sees it.

"There is no need to take this negatively. I admire your passion. The guilt that you heap upon yourself is an unnecessary burden. In this, your so-called savior is correct. But you must know that he delights in you carrying this burden. If you didn't, he would have nothing to save you from, taking away his own precious glory. And glory, which he admits in His own word, is what He wants most. Our father, on the other hand, would not have you live a life dedicated to his or another's glorification. He would share the spoils of battle with you."

"You're wasting your time, Agares. You're very clever—I'll give you that. But I'm not falling for this. Do you have any information for me?" I know I'm supposed to play along with him, but he's getting to me, and so I react defensively.

"Do you really believe that appearing clever is the limit of my desires? Revealing certain truths that I think you already know, yet fervently deny … that is my intent." He picks up on my clear agitation and continues gently, "Forgive me if I was too forward." His brow raises as he closes in on the glass. "So your beautiful lady is looking quite strong. She is primed to be quite the killer."

Now he's really getting to me. But I continue to resist the impulse to lose my cool. "Yes, she is. I'm glad you noticed."

"What are you willing to do for her?"

"Anything."

"Anything?" His voice is eerily soothing. "How about turning from your so-called savior? Would you do that?"

"Of course not." I begin to grind my teeth, holding back rage.

"Then it seems 'anything' is nothing more than mere sentiment." He pauses to wait for my answer. I have none. He continues, "The sad part is, He would have you turn your back on her for His sake, but turn your back on Him for her sake, even out of your true love for her, and what would your reward be? Eternal punishment. Am I the only one who sees a problem with this? 'The Lord gives and the Lord takes away,' yes? I would rather say that the Lord gives *so that* he may take away." He shows an expression that resembles sympathy. "Lucien, I'm trying to save you from the endless suffering that He subjects his children to. And I use that term loosely. If you fought for his majesty, then true happiness would be yours. Look around you. Who is sitting upon the throne, and who is living in the dust? His majesty would never subject you to this."

"No, he would just execute innocent civilians." Why am I arguing with this guy?

"And your Lord hasn't done the same? More than half of His word is filled with tales of His genocide, and all for the greater good, yes? I would submit that our father is doing the same thing. We serve masters that are more similar than you realize. Only my master would never threaten anyone with eternal punishment."

"That's because your master doesn't hold that power ... or that would be everyone's fate."

"Your Lord would have you believe that."

"My Lord speaks only truth, while yours is the father of lies." My voice is getting louder.

"Shall we talk about lies for a minute? Your Father cannot lie, correct?"

"That's right."

"And lying can be used as a weapon, can it not?"

"I suppose so."

"Okay, now if you were in a war, and you had a weapon that the enemy didn't have, wouldn't you use it to win the war?"

"Not if it meant betraying my God." The strength of my convictions calms me down.

"And why does it betray Him to lie or cheat ... or steal, for that matter? Simply because He cannot do it himself? It angers Him that beings He has created can do things that He cannot—and not only that, but that they can be used against Him. This angers Him so much that He sets up penalties for doing what He cannot do." His rock-solid steadiness only increases my agitation. He continues, "I don't know about you, but I wouldn't punish my own son if he could run faster than I could."

"He sets up penalties to protect us from the consequences. If I had a son who tried to jump off a cliff, I would punish him to save his life. And our Lord provides grace and forgiveness for all who disobey, even you."

He is unshaken and answers immediately, "Grace? Why do you think there is grace? I'll tell you why—because He has created a need for it, manipulating all of you into thinking that you need Him."

"I believe it was your master who created the need for grace. He convinced Eve to commit the first sin." I'm still arguing with him.

"He was opening her eyes and setting her free. It's not his fault your Lord killed his own children for breaking free."

"They had freedom from the beginning. Your master corrupted that freedom, and he continues to corrupt it."

He is silent.

"I'm not getting any information out of you, am I?" I say, remembering the reason I am talking with him in the first place. I step back from the glass and wait for an answer.

"I suppose you've earned some." He leans against the wall and slides back to sit. "If you travel approximately seventy-five miles at eighty-seven degrees from this base, you will find twenty-eight prisoners that are your people being held."

This information will most likely lead us into an ambush. "Thank you, but we'll see if you're telling the truth."

"Yes, we will," he answers, looking away from me as though I have now become an annoyance.

I'm so shaken, and he's done such a good job of getting into my head, that I have to quickly walk away. When I round the corner at the end of the hallway, I punch one of the metal doors in anger. Electric pain shoots up my arm, reminding me that I am unassigned at the moment. I walk farther down the hall, holding my hand and wincing. Zypher is waiting, and he can see that I'm flustered. "Sorry to subject you to that, Lucien, but I have confidence in the depth of your faith. That's why I allowed it. Did you get any information?"

"I think so. He said prisoners are being held seventy-five miles at eighty-seven degrees from our location, but who know if it's true or if it's just another ambush."

"Well, there's only one way to find out." Zypher looks down at my hand. "You okay?"

"Yeah, I don't think it's broken."

"All right. Well, I'm gonna put together a game plan for this mission. We should leave tomorrow, because we don't know how long this intel will be good."

Now I wish I hadn't said anything. I have very little faith in the trustworthiness of a man who works for Satan.

"In the meantime, I'd go see Tabitha if I were you. You may not see her for a while. Speaking of which, I just wanted to mention to you that we have a policy that married couples be stationed at the same base. If not, who knows when you'll see her again?"

"Wait. Are you saying I should ask her to marry me?" *Is my infatuation that obvious?*

He grins at me with a little laugh. "I'd wait on that for the moment, but don't wait too long, Lucien. Tomorrow is never promised us."

Later on, I am hastily searching the base for Tabitha. I don't know where to find her, so I start asking random people where she might be. I learn that she's in a room with those who are dying. When I enter the room, I hear a recording of peaceful sounds of the forest. It even smells like trees and fresh air. There are several beds with people in them hooked up to machines, some conscious, some unconscious. I see Tabitha seated in a chair beside one of the beds holding the hand of the occupant, an old woman. The sight of her giving such comfort makes her all the more beautiful to me. The old woman is chatting away about a boat and how she used to go sailing. Tabitha is just listening, nodding her head, and giving the woman her full attention. She hears my footsteps and turns around. Her smile brightens when our eyes meet. She waves me over to a chair next to her. I sit down as the woman continues talking. Tabitha gently interrupts her. "Ruth. Ruth. This is my friend Lucien."

I offer her my hand, and she takes it with a smile. "Well, he's a handsome young morsel, isn't he?"

"Ruth!" Tabitha blushes.

"What? I call 'em like I see 'em. Oh, and look—he glows too, just like you. You two make such a handsome couple."

"Oh, no, we're just friends," Tabitha says. This stings a bit, but I suppose it's my own fault. I haven't made my intentions known to her yet.

"Friends? Well, mister, you'd better do something to change that. All this beautiful young lady could do was talk about you before you came in."

"Ruth!"

Now Tabitha is covering her face.

"What? I call 'em like I see 'em." Ruth looks at me with the sweetest smile, as if she is certain that Tabitha and I are meant to be together. I'm literally praying at this moment that she's right. Tabitha and I seem very aware of how the other person is feeling, but are we just too shy to talk about it. Shy? I've never been the shy type. What's wrong with me?

We sit with Ruth for another hour or so, listening to her stories. Many of them are fascinating, and others seem to go nowhere and have no point. But the smile on her face tells us that she is just delighted to have someone care enough to listen to her. I know I'm doing a good thing, but it's exhausting. I look at Tabitha, and she isn't fazed. She seems to have a lot more patience than I do, which just makes me all the more attracted to her.

Ruth eventually says that she's tired and would like to go to sleep, so we say goodbye. We walk out together, content just to be in one another's presence again.

"Are you hungry?" Tabitha asks.

"Sure." We head to the cafeteria for a late dinner and talk for about two hours. I've never talked so easily and freely with anyone else. It's like God designed our personalities to blend in perfect harmony. I would give just about anything to stay in this moment with her. The idea that I'll have to leave her to go fight this stupid, never-ending war makes me want to weep in despair.

I walk her to her room at the end of the night. "Good night, Tabitha."

"Good night, dork."

I hold out my arms, offering a hug. She slowly embraces me, pressing her cheek to my chest. I don't want to let her go. I slowly exhale as peace and comfort flow through my body. After a while I realize that I may be holding her too long, so I loosen my embrace a little. I'm expecting her to let go, but she doesn't, so I squeeze her close again. We just hold each other for what feels like five minutes. Finally, we let go and stare deep into each other's eyes. It's the clearest I've ever seen her. She looks like an angel, and I can see the beauty of her pure heart. I want to kiss her badly, but I don't. I feel as though waiting on that will be a gift to both of us. So, I tear myself away from her and say good night. As I walk away, I'm thinking of anything and everything that could possibly prolong this precious night. I think of a random question to ask her and quickly turn around, but she's already in her room. Ah, well, I'll make sure to stop by in the morning to say goodbye.

CHAPTER

CAUTION IN THE WIND

ur meeting for a brief on our mission is the next morning at the fifth hour, and we're scheduled to leave at the seventh hour. We're all gathered in one of the common areas, which on this base are much more elaborate than they are on ours. They also have fireplaces, but they are twice the size, and the rooms are filled with personal recliners and beautiful paintings. A desert buffalo's head is mounted above the fireplace. I can't help but stare at it as everyone gathers for our briefing. Once we're all there, Zypher finally arrives. "All right, gents, so this is gonna be a tough one. As some of you may know, not only are we probably walking into an ambush, but our objective lies off the scorched third. We're heading into Babylon."

Looks of shock cover the other men's faces. After all we've been through, I'm wondering why this is a big deal.

"And as you all know, we can't be walking around with glowing faces in a populated area. The enemy would be all over us. We'll have to separate from our angels for a while and let them fight off the fallen that might follow us and give away our position."

Oh, that's why. I'm scared enough having to go into battle against demons while I have an angelic being at my side, but doing so without one seems unthinkable.

"Gentleman, I may be overstating the obvious, but even though we'll be without our angels, we will never be without the Son of God Himself."

This is where our faith is tested.

"Were the apostles assigned angels? Was Paul? No, but they completed their missions nonetheless."

Yeah, and save John, they were all executed. I know his words of comfort should help, but I'm ashamed to admit that they don't. I've become so dependent on my strength coming from Octavian, that I've forgotten where his strength comes from.

Although all of us are shifting in our seats, I've never seen Zypher more chipper. It's like his joy increases with danger. I just don't get it.

"So here's the plan. It's going to be obvious that we're not fallen, but not everyone out there is fallen. Many are just lost, so black eyes don't accompany them. So we're going to be posing as mercenaries, which isn't entirely false. After all, we're on an independent mission that must remain secretive, so refraining from talking specifics with anyone is a requirement either way. All right, all we have is a direction and a distance, so we're kind of winging it here. If we do find hostages, they become priority. If we can get out of there without fighting, it will be a bonus, but the enemy probably knows we're coming. We're not going to be able to bring our wrist weapons into a populated area. Security will most likely take them at the border, so we'll have to buy old-fashioned guns off the street. If we encounter 4D warfare, we'll have to surrender."

Excuse me? Did I just hear Zypher say 'surrender'?

"If we try to fight without our angels, we're dead for sure. If we surrender, we'll probably have to undergo some torture, but at least we'll have a chance of escape or rescue."

I can tell that no one, not even Tyrus, likes the sound of this. Zuriel raise his hand slowly like he's in grade school.

"What?" Zypher snaps.

Zuriel puts is hand down and protests, "Can I just say that this is the worst mission I've ever heard of?"

We all laugh nervously, trying to alleviate our fears with humor. Zypher looks at Zuriel with a smile that masks annoyance,

"Yes, you can. But if you say it again, I'll probably smack you in the mouth."

We all stop laughing.

"Yes, sir."

"What are you all so afraid of? If we die, we're with Him. If not, imagine the stories we'll have. You all should live for these kinds of missions. Okay, we step off in an hour and a half. Follow me into the prayer room, and I'll get an assigned priest to unassign us."

I'm already unassigned from the last battle, so I don't have to go, but the rest of the squad leaves.

I'm left alone in the common area, and my whole body is tense. We have no idea what we're walking in to, and our only information comes from one of the enemy. Well, I guess today is as good a day to die as any. If it weren't for wanting to spend more time with Tabitha, I probably wouldn't care so much. Knowing her somehow gives my life more value.

A half hour before we leave, Zypher leads us in prayer. Then, before I know it, we're patrolling in the dust, angel-less. I can't remember being on a patrol when we weren't attacked, so having to surrender seems highly probable. Miraculously, we walk for three days without being disturbed. It's almost like the enemy wants us to cross the border. Halfway through the fourth day, I can start to make something out in the distance. I can see haze and smell the beginnings of a foul odor. It smells like old sewage.

After another hour or two of walking, I can see columns of black smoke coming out of the haze, and the shapes of buildings. If this is what I think it is, then we are about to be pilgrims in an unholy land. It's the city where evil reigns, where God's wrath is destined to fall. It's the prostitute who rides the serpent. It's Babylon.

I've heard Tyrus talk about Babylon being on the border of the scorched third; and he's also said that God hasn't yet scorched it because a greater amount of His wrath is to be poured upon it in the future. He said that it could be recognized by its smell, and that he has never actually been there himself. Through other members of the squad, I have heard that the only one in our squad who has been there is Zypher, but no one knows in what capacity.

As we continue to walk, the buildings become clearer and the smell becomes stronger. The buildings are skyscrapers, surrounded by shorter buildings that are also tall. The city is surrounded by multiple layers of chain-link fence about fifty feet tall, topped with razor wire. Guard towers surround the city, making it look like a large prison from the outside. As we get closer, I'm haunted by the fact that there is no way to hide our approach. We approach one of the gates, and I can see that it is manned by six fallen, all assigned. If they suspect us, we are at their mercy. I can see they are smoking cigarettes and leaning against the fence, sitting and joking with one another. They see us and just give us a few mad dog looks before returning to their conversations. Zypher approaches the gate while the rest of us wait.

"Request twelve for entry."

The fallen man who appears to be in charge slowly stands, stretches his back, and walks up to Zypher on his side of the gated fence. He's a grizzly looking man with a shaved head and a beard. He has tattoos all over his head and forearms. His black eyes add to his lifeless presence. He stares at Zypher for a bit and then takes a drag off his cigarette and blows it in Zypher's face.

"What for?"

I tense up even more, as I'm waiting for Zypher to kick the gate open and break this guy's neck, which would certainly be the death of all of us. But he doesn't flinch.

"We're mercs, here for a bounty."

"Bounty, huh? Who you lookin' for?"

"None of your business." Zypher stands his ground.

Uh-oh.

"Oh, okay, well how 'bout this—" The fallen man's black cloak appears above him, and I about piss my pants. "You catch this bounty, and you bring half of the reward back here. Otherwise, I'll see that you're raped to death while you watch us kill your friends here."

Zypher's lack of expression amazes me. "That seems fair."

The fallen man stares at him, obviously angered that his threats have no effect. Then he smiles. "I really hope I see you again."

Then, to my surprise, he opens the gate.

"Drop your wrist weapons, and get your marks checked. Then you can enter."

We enter the gate, dropping our weapons as one of the fallen men pours rubbing alcohol from a clear bottle and wipes each of our foreheads to make sure our marks don't rub off. I hate to say it, but it's a good thing we had real marks forced upon us. They search each of us for more weapons and then let us through a few more gates. I'm guessing the only reason they didn't just kill us is because of the money that we could potentially bring them.

When we enter the final gate, we're immediately in a crowd of people, all going different directions. Most of them are dressed in suits and fancy clothes. They carry briefcases and are talking on coin-sized devices inserted in their ears. People are in such a hurry that they are running into one another, but strangely not caring and just continuing their fast-paced walking.

The skyscrapers are sparkling clean, yet raw sewage lines the gutters. I see a group of men in green jumpsuits cleaning up a grizzly scene of mangled dead bodies that seem to be the result of an auto accident. People in cars and on motorcycles zip through the streets, just passing by the bloody mess without even looking. The corners of the streets are piled high with garbage that's been lit on fire: the source of the columns of black smoke. The smell is horrific.

We have to jump in with the flow of the crowd and head in the general direction we were given. The population is so diverse that we are in no way conspicuous. Walking in the crowd is like getting caught in an unstoppable current. I have to put almost no effort into walking, because I'm getting pushed along. Occasionally, on the side of the street lies a dead, emaciated body. What's peculiar is that each dead body is dressed in nice clothes that just look worn. I'm expecting to see homeless people or beggars, but I see none—only bodies that everyone seems to ignore.

"What happened to these people?" I ask Zypher.

"They starved to death."

"What? How?"

"If you lose your job in a city that's lost all charity, you die of starvation. They find what they can in the trash, but it's never enough."

The picture of this place is becoming clear. A sick feeling is growing in me about what it must be like to live here. I am filled with further disgust as we pass stores advertising prostitutes of both sexes and all ages. I have to just keep walking. What can anyone do surrounded by such evil? Where is God? Does He not dwell in all of the Earth? Or did He just choose to withdraw His presence from this one city? Who's going to save these people? We're here to save hostages, but can we leave all these people like this? Then again, what could we possibly do?

I see looks of horror on the faces of the rest of the squad. Only Zypher maintains his sternness. He looks as though he's putting a great deal of effort into shutting it all out. He seems to have tunnel vision for where we need to go. He snaps at any of us who slow down to stare at the terrible things that surround us. He catches me stopped in front of an unhealthily skinny woman, crouched against a wall and crying. He grabs me by the collar.

"Move it! Shut all this out and focus! We came here for one reason."

"Yes, sir."

"We're gonna stop at the first pawnshop we see and get some guns."

We go into a store that's lined with guns on the back wall. It would be nice to have some heavy firepower, but we need something we can conceal, so we all get handheld pistols. Zypher pulls out gold coins from his pocket and pays the old man who runs the shop. He stares at Zypher with fear, as though he knows him, but Zypher just avoids his gaze.

We have to travel through a few more miles, and then the crowds begin to thin. More and more dead bodies litter the sides of the roads, and vultures surround them. It seems the cleanup crews don't visit the less-populated areas. The stench is unbearable. The most horrifying thing we see is a group of people dressed in suits and dresses, crouched over a dead body, all eating it with their bare hands. They all look up at us deeply fearful and broken. I have to look forward, or I'll vomit.

As we get farther away from the crowds, the buildings become shorter and most of them look abandoned. According to Tyrus, we've got only a few more miles to go until we reach our destination. This just seems too easy. Eventually, we're within a quarter mile of where Agares told us the hostages are being held. Zypher orders us to stop and spread out while taking cover. The objective looks like an abandoned convenience store, with two fallen men guarding the door. They haven't seen us yet, as we're hiding behind the corners of the adjacent buildings. Zypher peeks around the corner and then turns to us. "They're assigned."

There's no way we can fight them. We might as well just leave.

"I'm going to distract them. Tyrus, take your team inside once you're clear."

Tyrus looks confused. "Chief, I never argue with you, but that's just suicide."

"No, it's not. They won't kill me of they don't think I'm a threat. Trust me. Just slip in the door once they're distracted."

Zypher then starts ripping his shirt so it looks tattered. Then he reaches down and grabs some dirt and rubs it all over his face. He puts his pistol in the back of his pants and then stumbles toward the fallen men, pretending to be drunk.

"Hey, man!" he yells in a slurred voice. The men turn in surprise but then just smile when they see the state he appears to be in. I'm just watching, frozen because I can't believe what I'm seeing.

"I'm lookin' for a kitten named Jelly Bean. You seen her?"

He then proceeds to pee on the far side of their building, which prompts them to move.

"What are you doing, dipshit?" yells one of the men as they approach him. Then, faster than I can blink, I see Zypher draw his pistol and put two rounds into the forehead of each man. Both of their demons immediately come out of them in clouds of black dust and charge Zypher. Knowing what's coming, he throws his pistol just as the demons enter his nose and eyes. Tyrus gives us the motion to go and turns back to Zuriel before he follows us inside. "Hold him down, and make sure he doesn't do it!"

Zuriel's team rushes to Zypher, who's writhing on the ground now and grinding his teeth. Zuriel's team jumps on him, holding him down as we enter the building, weapons drawn. We clear the first room, which is empty besides a few wooden pallets. Tyrus kicks open the door to the next room, and immediately shots are fired. He returns fire as we enter the room, guns blazing. By the time I get in there, I see two unassigned men down, and I see Tyrus shoot the last man in the eye. He collapses like a rag doll, dead before he hits the ground.

"Let's go—next room."

He raises his pistol as we stack up against the next door. It's my turn to take point, so I kick the door in. The first thing I see is a cluster of very thin people all dressed in brown. They all have fresh marks on their foreheads and range in age from about twenty to fifty. There are around twenty of them, all shaking in the corner of the dusty concrete room. I can see a few dead bodies stacked in the other corner, also dressed in brown. Who knows how long they've been locked in here. I suddenly hear a lot of shooting and yelling outside. My instinct is to run out and help, but Tyrus firmly grabs my arm.

"There may be assigned fallen out there. If we go out, we're all dead."

He then addresses the whole team. "Let's get these people out a side door and see if we can get an idea of the situation out there."

He then looks to the group of thin people. "I know you're confused and exhausted, but you're going to have to trust us. We're here to save you."

He motions for the people to follow us as we climb out a window. Once we help them and hide them behind an adjacent building, Tyrus tells me to creep around the side of the building to see what's going on.

As I peer around the corner, I see eight members of our squad surrounded by twenty to thirty assigned fallen. Floating men surrounded by glowing black cloaks encircle them as men on the ground bind them with shackles. There's nothing we can do.

I go back to Tyrus and tell him. He checks it out for himself and returns, sterner than I've ever seen him. "All right, let's finish this mission and get these people out of here. We'll have to come back later for the squad."

We know he hates the taste of the words as he says them, and we all want to protest, but we know fleeing is our only choice. Besides, Tyrus is now in charge. We start quickly shuffling the people along from building to building, hoping the enemy isn't close behind. We can hear someone being tortured as we leave.

Screams we can do nothing about will haunt us for some time to come.

The people are so pale and emaciated that I'm surprised they can even walk. Any will of their own that they once had has been beaten down by whatever horrors they've just gone through. They follow us blindly and just stare at the ground. I'm thinking I have no idea what we're going to do with these people. Even if we can miraculously get them out of the city, they'll never survive the walk back.

We slowly move from building to building until we're about a mile away from the fallen. All the people we rescued have to sit down to rest. Tyrus herds them into an abandoned building and tells me and Alcyone to go into town to get them some food and water. We double-time it back into the crowded area and find a little store that sells tacos. We buy sixty tacos and forty bottles of water and double-time it back to where Tyrus is waiting. We pass out the food and water until there's none left. Although the people are starving, they eat slowly, as though they'd forgotten how. Tyrus looks at me and puts his hands palms up with a shrug.

"What, you didn't get me any? I like tacos too." I look at him confused, and he punches me in the shoulder. "I'm just messin' with you, bro."

Only a guy like Tyrus could maintain a sense of humor in a situation like this. I look at how slowly the people are eating, and I want to tell them to hurry up, but I can't bring myself to do it.

"All right, everyone, we have to get moving, so you'll have to finish later," declares Tyrus, finally.

I feel like a sitting duck just waiting here.

"The sooner we can get back in the heart of the city, the sooner we'll be safe. It'll be easier to hide," says Tyrus as he starts helping people up one by one. We get back out on the street and start moving from building to building again. We make sure the coast is clear before crossing open areas. Once we see crowds of people again, we stop moving covertly and just walk among them

"Where are we headed?" I ask Tyrus.

"Still figuring that out." He talks quietly so only I can hear him. "The fences around the city go ten feet deep, and they're patrolled by assigned fallen. I'm thinking a leap of faith may be in order."

"A leap of faith?"

"Yeah. We're gonna have to just walk these people right out the front. It's the last thing they'll be expecting."

"But they'll recognize us."

"Not if we wait until night when a different shift is on duty. We'll tell them we've been hired to clean up the city and take those about to die out into the dust so their bodies won't pollute the city. It's less work for them, so hopefully they'll just let us go. Let's just pray that they don't all communicate well with each other."

"Yeah, won't they be looking for us?"

"I guess we'll find out."

Anytime I think it can't get any scarier, it does. I'm actually starting to get used to it.

"I didn't see anything that resembled a motel when we were in the city. We're just gonna have to wander around until they change the guards at the front gate."

I look back at the people we've rescued, and I see a couple of them vomiting. I go to check on them to make sure they're okay. One is a middle-aged woman, and the other is a teenage boy. They must have eaten too fast. Their stomachs have obviously shrunk from the lack of food.

"Are you okay?" I ask them. Dumb question. They just look at me with blank stares and then look back at the ground.

"I'm sorry I wasted the tacos, sir," the kid tells me.

"Hey, buddy, don't even worry about it. We can get more later." He smiles.

We make our way to the front gate to see if the guards have changed. When we get in visual range, we can see that they haven't. So we spend the next few hours wandering around the city. I would have hoped that I would be used to the stench by now, but it's as pungent as ever. The filth of the city, both physically and spiritually, seems to put a dark cloud over all of us. We start getting into little arguments about which way to go. I start losing my patience and snapping at the people we've rescued, telling them to stay with the group, because they keep wandering off. I shouldn't blame them in the state they're in, but the disgust and tension of this city make us all short-tempered.

We see several fights break out as we walk around. I can't even figure out how they start. People must not like the look of each other. Who knows? All I can think about is the rest of the squad and if they're even alive. And if they are, what's happening to them? It makes me sick that we just left them there. I have to keep reminding myself that we had no choice.

The more people keep bumping into me, the more I hate them and their disgusting city. I just want to get out of here. The sun finally starts to set, and we head back to the front gate. Thankfully, the guard has changed out and new fallen are posted, so they won't recognize us. As we approach the gate to exit, the guards give us strange looks. Tyrus takes the lead. A short, stocky assigned fallen man comes up to the gate and faces Tyrus. "Yeah?"

"Requesting exit," Tyrus says.

"Where you headed?" The man's raspy voice grates against my ears.

"Disposing of some dying trash here." He gestures to the people we have with us.

"Really?" The man opens the gate and lets us through. "So you wouldn't be on some kind of humanitarian rescue mission, would you?"

Tyrus laughs. "What for? I got my own problems. We're just doing what we're paid to do."

The fallen man stares at Tyrus for a second, searching his eyes. "Okay, so if you're just doing disposal, then you won't mind if I do this …"

The fallen man points his wrist weapon at the teenage boy I was talking with earlier and shoots him in the face. I jump back in shock but suddenly realize I have to restrain myself. Tyrus just shakes his head as though someone had scratched the paint on his car.

"Now, what did you go and do that for? Now I have to carry this garbage."

Tyrus puts the boy over his shoulder and walks toward the next gate. The fallen man seems satisfied with his response and lets the rest of us go through. He motions to the next gate to let us through also. I'm praying no one else gets killed as we walk out into the dust.

Once we're out of visual range of the city, we bury the boy. Tyrus apologizes to him with tears in his eyes as he covers him with the last bit of dust.

"All right, gents, we're heading back to the healing base. We gotta get a rescue squad together ASAP and head back to the city."

None of us wants to go back there, but we also can't leave the squad to their fate.

I speak up. "Wait, how? It'll take a whole company of elite assigned just to enter the city, unless we're going back in unassigned?"

I should have kept my mouth shut, but this seems impossible. Tyrus gives me a look that tells me to know my place, so I keep quiet. "All right, let's move."

We begin the journey back to the healing base, praying we're not attacked on the way.

The walk back is the most excruciating trek I've ever experienced. I can't even imagine what it must be like for these malnourished, dehydrated people, who are just clinging to life.

It's amazing how much weight emotional stress can press on your back when you have to move. I can sense that we all feel like cowards for leaving our friends to a fate of such suffering. Selfishly, I think about how hard it's going to be to have to face the other warriors on base and tell them that we've left the rest of our squad to be tortured and probably killed. And it wasn't even my call. I look toward Tyrus, who is leading the squad. I can see only the back of his head, but I picture the somber look on his face and wonder about the guilt he must be feeling.

"Halt!" I hear from the back. Another person has collapsed. Our new companions keep falling behind, and some of them even pass out. Each time it happens we have to stop, as none of us is assigned and therefore we don't possess the strength to carry another human being for hours on end. As soon as passed-out people are revived, we give them water and immediately keep moving. We don't have time for rest, and the fallen in Babylon have more than likely discovered what happened by now. Although Zypher and the rest of the squad are the toughest men I have ever known, even they have their breaking points.

In the middle of the second day, an elderly woman passes out and hits the dust face-first. As this is becoming routine, I go to wake her up without being alarmed. I shake her and pour water on her face. Nothing. I try a few more times and notice that her face has gone completely pale and she's no longer breathing.

"Tyrus!" I yell, not knowing what do to given our circumstances. He comes running, and seeing her condition he begins CPR. After a few minutes without success he pulls out a small shovel and begins digging. He notices me doing nothing and looks at me. "Well? Are you gonna help, or what? If they find her, they can track us."

I feel ill, but I follow orders. This is too much death for one mission. I thought that I would be numb to it at this point, but it feels like a wound that just gets deeper every time someone dies. Several of the people cry as we bury her. I learn that her

126

name was Rebecca. I don't even have the energy to dwell on the question Could I have done more? I just don't want anyone else to die. I take Tyrus to the side and beg him to slow down, but he insists that doing that could mean all of our deaths. His orders seems so cold to me, but I also know that he's right.

Taking mercy on everyone, he allows us to stop for sleep, but only for a few hours.

I'm awoken by the sound of thunder. I feel sick when I wake up, as though sleeping only made me more tired. There's lightning in the sky but no clouds or rain. It's actually quite beautiful, and I stop to admire it as Tryus wakes everyone else up. The shape of the lightning bolts grow as they strike, like rapidly growing roots. I start to wonder what God is thinking as He makes such things. Are they for our benefit? Are they for us to enjoy? Or does He just like playing with electricity and reminding us how small we are? Whatever His reasoning, it's a brilliant display of power, and I feel honored to witness it. I wish I could just revel in this experience and not have to face the realities before me. Being reminded of His presence and the eternity that awaits me with Him makes these present trials seem small. Thank you, Lord.

We quickly get back on the move, and our new friends are as tired as ever. The frequent stops continue, but we don't lose anyone else. My hope stays alive that we will make it back.

CHAPTER

RETURN TO BABYLON

e never know where we are or when we'll arrive until suddenly we do, and it's as though we are jolted awake out of this never-ending dream of dry heat and dust. By the grace of God we have made it back without being attacked. Once we have descended into safety, we hand the hostages over, limping and collapsing, for treatment and rehabilitation.

"Don't get too comfortable," Tyrus says as he quickly departs. I can only assume he's gone to report our situation and request permission to carry out a rescue mission.

In the meantime, I do everything I can to find Tabitha, since this may be the last time I see her. After looking absolutely everywhere, I give up and sit in a common area, staring at the fire and praying I get to see her one last time. With the squad stuck in Babylon, I know the mission isn't over. I watch the fire lick around the logs, and I escape into the peace of the flames.

It's her silhouette that catches my eye on the other side of the fire. As Tabitha's face comes into focus, I realize she hasn't seen me yet, but she has a look of defeat on her face that reminds me of how I felt when I was trying to find her. I sit up a bit taller as she gets closer. She sees me. Surprise fills her face as she runs into my arms and then punches me in the stomach. I double over in pain. She's forgotten that she's assigned and I'm not.

"What was that for?" I wheeze.

"I've been looking everywhere for you, you jerk!"

No wonder I couldn't find her. It makes me happy, but it doesn't take away the enormous amount of physical pain that I'm in. She suddenly realizes how hard she hit me and quickly bends down to pick me up. "Ooohhh, I'm sorry! I forgot you were unassigned."

She picks me up and holds me close. It was almost worth getting hit to be comforted like this. Tears start to roll down her face. "I didn't know if you were coming back. I was so scared. Don't leave again, okay? There are plenty of elite squads who can go on that rescue mission."

Word travels fast.

"Tabitha, you know I can't leave my squad there."

She slowly exhales, but she doesn't let me go. "I know. Well, then I'm going with you."

"Tabitha, we're not civilians anymore. These decisions are not ours to make. Besides, this is a mission you want to sit out, believe me."

She backs up a bit and gives me a look of disappointment. "Oh, please. You've seen what I can do."

"Okay, good point. But do you really want to go in unassigned?"

Another disappointed look. "Lucien, where's your faith? Even without angels, He's with us."

I swear, if I have to hear that one more time ...

"Okay, so if He's with us, then why did only half of us make it back? Why are they being tortured as we speak? If He's with us, then He's choosing not to help."

I can see her back off as I get angrier. "All right, I don't know what you've just been through, but I just want to be with you and help."

Her gentleness calms me immediately.

"I know. I'm sorry. Please forgive me. I haven't slept well in days."

"It's all right."

She hugs me again. The beauty of these moments is that I want them to never end. The tragedy is that they do. Just then, Tyrus comes in and tells me we have a meeting. Tabitha and I share one more glance as we let our hands go and I march off to duty.

Tyrus is walking at a rapid speed. I follow him to a room where the rest of the squad is waiting. He quickly addresses us. "Okay, gents, I talked it over with some higher-ups, and we have a few options. There's the good old-fashioned frontal assault, but as Lucien mentioned, it would take an entire company just to breech the perimeter, and we'd lose more men than we'd save. Another option would be to go back in unassigned, but then we'd stand no chance against any assigned fallen, which are sure to be holding them. Now, as you all know, only priests can assign us, so our best and only option is to take a priest in with us. But the problem is that no priests are available on this base, we don't have the time for a trek back to our base, and time is running out. I'm honestly at a loss, so I'm open to any ideas."

We're all silent for a few moments. Sergios slowly raises his hand.

"What do you got, Sergios?" asks Tyrus with a sense of urgency.

"We could try Kratos."

"What? No way. He's been out of commission for years. He's not even allowed to assign people anymore. What else?"

He looks around at all of us, and we are silent.

"I don't think we have another option, chief," says Sergios.

Tyrus exhales and drops his head, knowing that Sergios is

right. "All right. But just so you all know, we're gonna have to do this under the radar, since I know the higher-ups would never have it. I'm probably gonna lose rank over this."

He pauses and looks around as though he's stalling for time.

"Okay, screw it. Everybody follow me." He quickly walks out of the room, shaking his head but knowing this is our only option. We all follow. As we follow him through halls and down stairways, he looks around as though he's about to be caught doing something wrong. My curiosity gets the better of me, and I walk next to him to find out who this Kratos is.

"So, Tyrus, who is this guy?"

"He used to be a priest but was caught banging a girl he was supposed to be assigning. He's also an alcoholic. After that incident they stripped him of his title, and now he works in the kitchen as a dishwasher."

"You're joking, right? So how is he supposed to help us?"

"I doubt that he can, but we've got no other choice. We have to at least try."

We walk for about another fifteen minutes down more and more staircases until we reach a door that has a "Do Not Disturb" sign hanging on the door handle like it's a hotel room. Tyrus looks at it and chuckles. He pounds on the door with the back of his fist several times. There's no answer. He does it again even harder. I can hear a mumbled voice from inside. *"Whaaat?"*

"Kratos, it's Tyrus! Open up!"

"No!"

"If you don't open the door, I'm kicking it down," Tyrus says matter-of-factly.

"I don't have your money! Come back tomorrow!"

Tyrus looks at me as though he doesn't want to do what he's about to do. He shrugs his shoulders and then faces his back to the door. He violently mule-kicks the door, and his foot goes right through it but doesn't open it. Now he gets really frustrated, yanks his foot out, and kicks the hole open bigger and bigger.

"Hey, man! *Who's gonna fix that, you friggin ass?*" says Kratos from the inside.

When the hole is finally big enough to crawl through, Tyrus climbs in and tells us to follow. When I climb in, all I can smell is BO, old beer, and cigarette smoke. Seated in a recliner is a chubby older man smoking a cigarette, wearing boxers and a white-stained tank top.

"Hey, gents. How you all doin'?" he says in a slurred voice. He reaches for a bottle of wine on the nightstand next to him and takes a huge swig.

"You boys want a drink?"

"Kratos, we don't have much time, but you need to get dressed and come with us now," says Tyrus.

"Where we goin'? Dancing?" He laughs.

"I don't have time to explain, but you need to come with the four of us into Babylon and assign us inside the city."

"Hell, no. The last time I was in Babylon a Chinese hooker took my money and ditched me. No way am I going back there."

"Look, the fallen are holding our friends hostage, and we can't go in unassigned, or they'll destroy us. You're the only one who can help us."

"Come on. You know I can't assign anymore. I'll get in serious trouble." He burrows deep into his recliner and sucks down a long drag from his cigarette.

"What are they gonna do, demote you?"

Kratos laughs at this. "All right, fine. But if we make it out alive, you owe me a month's worth of drinks, and you gotta start inviting me to your poker nights again."

"Sure, fine. Let's just go. Now." Tyrus has already started opening drawers and throwing clothes at him.

"Well hold on to your britches. Let me get some coffee and put some pants on … in that order."

I can see Tyrus losing his patience. "Hurry up about it."

Kratos slowly takes his time making coffee and getting

dressed as Tyrus glares at him the entire time. I get the feeling if we didn't need him so much that Tyrus would have knocked him out by now. There are times when circumstances are so dire and the stress level is so high, yet something hilarious unfolds right in the middle of it. This instance is one of those times.

I bite my tongue until it bleeds to keep from laughing. I let out a snort, and Tyrus slowly turns to me, eyebrows raised as if to say, *Excuse me?*

"Sorry," I say quickly as I step back out of his punching range. Then after all that, Kratos makes his coffee and sits in his recliner to drink it. At this point I'm waiting for Tyrus to choke him out, but to my surprise, he doesn't move. He just looks at me. His eyes widen as though he can't believe what's happening, and he shakes his head.

When Kratos has finished his coffee, we head out and gear up. As we walk to the tunnel to begin our vertical climb, we get curious looks from officers who can't help but notice a drunken Kratos with us. One of them tries to engage Tyrus in conversation, but Tyrus just ignores him and walks faster. I know we are all going to have to answer for this if and when we make it back, but I don't care.

The thought of Zypher and my brothers in the hands of the enemy makes all that concern go away. Just before we reach the tunnel, I see Tabitha. Our eyes meet, and she runs toward me. My instinct is to run toward her, but I catch myself and just keep walking. She catches up to me and grabs my shoulder. "Hey, dork, where you guys going?"

"Just a training thing. We'll be back soon."

Tyrus gives me a look that says, *Get rid of her.*

"Can I come watch?"

"No, sorry. I'll see you soon though."

I try to walk away, but she keeps following. "Wait. Why is he with you guys?" She gestures toward Kratos.

"Oh, he's just gonna watch."

I can see the wheels in her head turning. "Are you going on that mission?"

"What? I gotta go. I'll talk to you soon."

"I'm coming."

"No, you're not," I whisper sharply, indicating for her to keep her voice down.

"If you're going to fight, I'm going with you. I won't lose you. You can't stop me."

Since she's assigned at the moment and the rest of us aren't, she's actually right. We couldn't stop her if we tried. Tyrus, knowing we don't have time for this and realizing that we could actually use her, looks at me and gives me a reluctant nod. She sees this.

"Yes!" She jumps in the air and then hugs me.

"Shhh!" I say into her ear as she squeezes me.

"Sorry. Is this secret or something?"

"I'll explain later, but just know you're gonna be in huge trouble when we get back here."

She looks me deeply in the eyes. "I don't care."

"Let's go!" Tyrus barks at us. We snap out of it and start walking again.

As much as I love that Tabitha is with me, I suddenly find myself worrying about her safety. I'm looking at her beautiful profile as we walk, and I am tortured by the thought of anything happening to her. I know she is a warrior, but I still feel the need to protect her with my life.

I love her.

I want to tell her in that moment, but I know it's not the right time.

When we get to the surface, Tyrus tells Kratos to reassign himself so he can assign all of us before we reach the city in case of 4D warfare on the way. His plan is to unassign all of us before we get within visual range of the gate and hope it goes unnoticed in the fourth dimension.

Kratos kneels and mumbles to God in his slurred voice. I'm expecting nothing to happen, but to my surprise his skin begins to glow. I guess assigning is a gift you never lose regardless of what you've done. He then reassigns all of us. Surely this cannot go unnoticed on the surface. But somehow it does. Someone must be watching over us.

As soon as we're done, Tyrus steps it out without a word, and we all follow. It feels so right to be assigned again. Within a mile we have to stop because Kratos is puking his guts out. Tyrus, showing patience beyond what I knew he had, silently waits next to him. We keep going at an unbelievable pace. Kratos falls back several times, and I have to grab the strap of his pack and drag him along. When I get tired of doing that, I tell him to grab the back of my pack and I tow him like a dead car. I never thought that I could get exhausted from hiking while being assigned, but the combination of the pace we're going and having to drag Kratos is really testing my endurance.

After about twelve hours, we finally stop. I'm catching my breath when suddenly the wind picks up. We look up to see the familiar black faces forming in the sky. Tabitha is the first to attack. She takes out two demons with her jackhammer attack. I see another coming at her from the flank, and I quickly intercept it, destroying it. Tyrus is ricocheting from demon to demon, leaving screaming black dust in his wake. Within minutes we kill at least thirty, with no losses to ourselves. In the aftermath we're all gasping for air, and we notice Kratos seated in the dust, smoking a cigarette. We all look at him.

"What?" he says. "I don't fight. But that was pretty gnarly, I must say."

He takes another drag off his cigarette and ignores the fact that we are all staring at him. We have no choice but to let it go. After all, he is the most valuable asset in our squad at the moment. Looking at him seated in the dust, staring off into the distance, makes me wonder what pain he carries. Whatever he feels, he covers it well with his black humor and careless demeanor, but all I have to do is look into his eyes for a second, and his scars become grossly apparent. It's as though he knows God has forgiven him for his shortcomings, but that he disagrees with God's decision and refuses to forgive himself. I would reach out to him if I had even the slightest notion of how to do so, but I hesitate, as I only anticipate a cold response. I recognize my empathy and immediately try to stuff it, knowing it will only distract me from the mission at hand. I suppose pondering the wounds on Kratos' heart is a good distraction from imagining what Zypher and the others might be going through ... and wondering if the same fate awaits us.

To my enormous disappointment, Tyrus barks at us all to keep moving. He promises he will allow us to rest as soon as we're clear of the combat zone. About thirty minutes later, he is true to his word and gives the welcomed signal to stop. The rest of us fall in the dust, not even bothering to take our gear off. Tyrus calmly and with very deliberate movements sets up his sleeping area and scans the perimeter.

In vain I try to emulate his energy and discipline, but I find myself too exhausted to move that fast. I have no doubt that if we get attacked right now, we will all be killed for lack of strength.

I suddenly wonder how Kratos is even alive after all this. I look over and see him sleeping in the dust, using his pack as a pillow. Ah, well, he'll wake up when it gets cold. At least he didn't have a heart attack. As I'm setting up my sleeping area, Tabitha comes over to me, looking just as exhausted as I feel, but with a joy underneath her eyes that I wish I had the privilege of possessing.

"How are you holding up?" she asks me. I should be asking her that question.

"I don't know how we made it through that. Tyrus is a beast," I respond.

She just smiles at me with droopy eyes and slowly embraces

me. It actually makes me a little uncomfortable that I have the ability to ignite such joy in her, because I see so much wrong with my own heart. It makes me question her judgment.

Either way, I am eternally grateful to have affection from such a precious human being. I look around to see if anyone is watching, and they are all racked out—minus Tyrus, who is walking the perimeter of our camp. I know I should let Tabitha sleep while she has the chance, but I just can't bring myself to let her go. We hold each other in beautiful silence for what seems like hours. I break the silence.

"Don't you want to sleep?"

"Not if I have to let you go."

No person save Jesus Christ Himself has ever made me feel so loved.

"If this is our last night on Earth, I'm glad I get to spend it with you." Her words melt me.

I don't think I've ever really been in love until now. The memories I have of being what I thought was in love pale in comparison to this. Never before have I truly known at the bottom of my heart that I would give my life for a woman. But I would gladly place mine upon the altar for Tabitha. We stare at the glowing outline of the moon through the gray sky. Reluctantly, we let go of one another and lock eyes. She can see all of me, and I can see all of her. I know that I may die tomorrow, so I slowly move toward her and softly kiss her. I can feel her body relax in my arms as our lips meet. She lets out the gentlest sigh of pleasure, which is like music to my soul. Electricity runs through my body as though I'd just been injected with some sort of euphoric drug. God, please let me live in this moment forever.

"I love you, Tabitha." I don't care that I said it first.

"I love you, Lucien."

We both understand that nothing more needs to be said, and we go to our respective sleeping areas to get what is perhaps our last night of rest. I'm out the moment my body hits the ground.

A welcoming cool breeze greets me at the top of a mountain. Bright green, rolling hills with scattered giant redwoods are a feast for my eyes. Breathing the pure air is healing to my soul. I look down and see a cliff face beneath me, but I am so at peace that I am unafraid. Through the valley before me runs a wide, winding river, flowing and feeding the green life that surrounds it. The warmth of the sun in the clear blue sky fills me with life-giving comfort from the outside in. In the distance behind me, I can hear some rustling in the leaves. Something is moving in my direction, but I can't see what it is through the bushes and trees. Excitement and anticipation well up within me as the sounds get closer. I hope it is what I think it is. A figure emerges from the shadows that fulfills my expectation. Octavian's smiling face is exposed to the sunlight, prompting me to run to him. Although I'm fairly certain that this is a dream, part of me is hoping that I've been killed in combat so I won't ever have to leave this place.

"Sorry, buddy. You're not dead yet." I had forgotten that he could hear my thoughts.

I smile. "Well, maybe next time."

We share a chuckle and then embrace.

"So how's it goin', my friend? You hangin' in there?" he asks.

"I think so, but I gotta admit, I don't have a whole lotta faith that this particular mission will succeed," I respond.

"Yeah, I hear you. And so what if it doesn't? Then you can spend as much time here as you want, not to mention walking with J Himself!"

The thought of it crumbles me. To walk with my savior for all eternity forces tears of joy from my eyes. I sob at the shame of wanting my life on Earth to end already.

"Hey, hey …" Octavian puts his hand on my shoulder.

He continues, "All God's warriors on Earth have come to this point. To desire to be with the Father more than you desire to be in the world is a good place to be, brotha. It's nothing to be ashamed of. In hindsight it will seem like a very short time when you're finally there."

His words comfort me and remind me once again how minimal my current suffering is in comparison to the joy yet to come. I look up at Octavian, who is giving me the look a father would give his son after he had skinned his knee. It brings me comfort that penetrates all the worry and anxiety that's been building in me over the last few days.

"Come on. Let's go sit down and enjoy the view." He helps me to my feet, and we walk over to the edge of the cliff, take a seat, and let our legs dangle over the side.

"Do you know why He made all of this?"

I know the answer, but I want to hear him say it.

"Because He loves you. He knew the expression of love you would feel when your eyes soaked in such beauty."

"Why does He love us so much? How can He love hearts so full of rebellion and evil?"

"Well, I could quote His word to you, but you've already heard those answers. When you see His face someday, only then will you truly understand. But to simply know that He does love you like He does, even without fully understanding why, should lead you to ultimate peace."

And it does. I don't need all the answers; I just long for more understanding so I can love like He does.

"Hey, trying to love like He does is like trying to become the sun simply by soaking in its rays. He *is* love. Someday He will bring you to perfection, but He will never cease to be the true source of all love that exists."

Peace fills my soul. To know that I will never have to love without Him takes a burden off my shoulders.

We spend the next few minutes in peaceful silence, just swimming in the joy of our surroundings. It dawns on me how amazing it is that someone as ancient as Octavian, who must have seen all the Earth had to offer through all of its ages, can still enjoy something as simple as a beautiful view. It begins to prompt many questions in my mind about Octavian's history. I know that he is aware of my questions before I even ask them. He looks at me and smiles. "Well, what do you want to know first? How old I am? What I've seen? Do I have feelings?

He laughs.

"I'm a living soul just like you, Lucien. Our Father made us both and gave us both free will. I'm just a different species, so to speak, in terms of souls. If you were to see me in my spirit form and stand next to me in your spirit form, you would know our differences clearly. I can't really describe them using simple English words, but if you were to combine the concepts of color, shape, and feeling into one term, that is how we would differ. Granted, this can't be done in the third dimension, but you'll see someday."

He smirks at me, sensing my confusion.

I ask my next question. "So why were you made, and why were you made before us?"

"Well, you and I were made for the same reason: to live in eternal communion with our Father and to glorify Him."

"But why does He need glory?"

"He doesn't, but the act of glorifying Him is what defines that communion. He takes joy in it, and He takes joy in the fact that we enjoy it. A characteristic of love is a desire to share itself and He, being as great and perfect as He is, could not share that love without being worshipped and revered."

For the first time in my life, glorifying God is not such a mystery. It makes perfect sense.

"As for why we were made first … well, only He knows the full answer to that one. But ask yourself this: do you think you have the ability to minister to angels?"

"Of course not."

"So then, doesn't it make sense that He made us first? So we could be your helpers?"

His answer doesn't fully satisfy my curiosity.

"Hey, buddy, it's the best you're gonna get for now." He laughs again. "Okay, I know you have other questions, so go ahead."

"Okay, how old are you?"

He cracks a smile and then looks off into the horizon.

"Well, that's a tough one. I'm older than the Earth, but when God made the Earth, He gave time its meaning. Before that it had no measure or meaning. The worlds, dimensions, and battles that I've experienced are things I can't describe to you while you possess the limited capacity for understanding you currently do. I promise you that I will describe all of them in detail someday when He gives you your new mind and your new body. But for now, let's just say that I am older than you, and God is older than both of us."

Once again, my curiosity is unsatisfied. Octavian pauses in thought for a few seconds.

"Why do you think Jesus spoke to you in parables and metaphors? Just to play a sick game? It was because they were the best way He could describe the things of His kingdom to humans who have never heard, seen, or even imagined the reality of such things. Why do you think He allows you to have children? Or a spouse? So you can understand in your terms just a taste of the love He has for you. Now, before you ask your next question, let me give you its answer. He will be fully present in His true form with you someday. Why He isn't now and why you can't see things as clearly as you'd like all have to do with the fall. Man has not been fully right with Him since. As you well know, Jesus is the only way to get right with Him again. And the reason you continue to live with the burdens and sorrows that you do, even after you've accepted Him, is that He is preparing you for war, among other things."

"War?"

"That's right. What do you think Revelation is all about? Cotton candy and sleigh rides?"

"So we have to fight wars here, die, and then fight more wars?"

"Well, one war."

"Will it ever end?"

He begins to look frustrated.

"You need to pick up your Bible, son. Yes, it ends. But you have more missions yet to come that have more significance than you will ever know in this life. And the qualities and character that are being developed in you now will play a huge role in the success of those missions. Do you really think the fruits of the spirit have significance for only this short life? Absolutely not. Their worth is eternal. Paul said that knowledge would pass away, but he never said anything about the fruits of the spirit passing away."

He is blowing my mind right now. I'm trying to imagine what these "missions" might be.

"Stop right there," says Octavian. "Trying to think practically about the things I've just told you with your mind is like trying to fly simply by running faster—it's not gonna happen. My point in telling you these things is I want you to know that all of your pains, sorrows, struggles, and joys hold eternal significance. You follow me?"

"Yeah, I do," I say as I lower my head, saddened by my own lack of faith and understanding. He pauses as if to decide if he should tell me what he's about to tell me next.

"He's proud of you and the man you've become. At least take peace in that."

I look at him in shock as tears well up in my eyes. I let my face fall into my hands and weep. If the Father Himself is proud of who I am, then why am I so disappointed in myself? Octavian scoots over and puts his arm around my shoulder.

"You're just becoming more aware of the weight of your own sin. Believe it or not, this is a good thing. It means His light is shining on you more and more. Accept the power of His blood. Accept His love. Know that in Him, you are clean and blameless."

I can't stop crying. He just pulls me closer to him and pats my shoulder in comfort, knowing I have to let this out. When I finally expend all the tears I have in me, I look up at the view and am reminded once again of how much He truly does love me. I feel a warmth engulf my heart, and I sit in peace. We sit in silence for a while as new questions begin to surface in my mind. I hesitate to ask them, as I am afraid of the answers. I take the opportunity anyway. "Is all of this worth it to Him? I mean, all the pain and sorrow?"

"I think you know the answer to that, my friend, but yes, absolutely it is. He would have written you off as a failed experiment thousands of years ago if it wasn't."

I think of all the answers I've been seeking, this one is the most satisfying. It puts all of my other questions to rest. Octavian can sense this and looks over at me with a Fatherly smile. He pats me on the back and stands.

"Well, I would love to stay here just as much as you would, but as you know, we have work to do."

I look up to answer him, but he's gone. I can feel the pain in my stomach slowly return, as I know this moment has to end and I must wake. I close my eyes to enjoy one more breath of the fresh mountain air.

As I open my eyes, they are heavy. I can open them only halfway before they close again. The sting of the cold grows on my feet and face, and I realize that I'm shivering. I'm awake. It's still dark, but I look over and see that Tyrus is already up and ready to move. Did he even sleep? He's stuffing his sleep sack into his pack and acknowledges me without even looking at me.

"Mornin', sunshine. Sleep well?"

"Oh, yeah," I mumble.

"All right, gents, let's get moving!"

The urgency of his voice makes my whole body ache, knowing I have to move much faster than I want to. As I fully wake up, the leftover peace and comfort I experienced in my dream wear off. I pack my gear as quickly as I can.

"Hey, stranger. Long time no see." The sound of her voice is as welcoming as ever. I look up from what I'm doing and see Tabitha, packed and ready to go. I'm an expert at this sort of routine. How did she get ready faster than I did? I guess she's just a natural. I quickly hug her and get back to packing, not wanting to arouse Tyrus's anger by stalling. As I finish packing, I throw my gear back on, give Tabitha a quick smile that tells her I can't stop thinking about the previous night, and fall into formation.

After a few hours, I begin to smell the familiar stench of the putrid welcome that Babylon offers all of its visitors. Tyrus halts us, indicating that we are getting close to visual range of the city.

"All right, Kratos, do your thing," he orders.

Kratos unassigns each of us in turn, and unassigns himself last. Tyrus quickly motions all of us in for a last-minute huddle. As we run toward him, I realize we never took the time to discuss even an outline of a plan. What are we going to do, and how are we going to get into the city? Even with us unassigned, they will be looking for us and perhaps even expecting us. The insanity of what we are attempting hits me, and I fill with fear.

"All right, gents, here's the plan. We're merchants meeting with food vendor owners in order to negotiate a deal for cheaper food delivery." He pauses and looks at each of us. We look at each other in silence, clearly unimpressed by his plan.

"Well, any of you turds have a better idea?"

Silence.

"All right then, let's go. Leave your weapons here. Bury them, and take note of the coordinates," he says, moving back into formation without another word. After obeying orders, we follow, knowing no amount of creativity will get us past the gates. It's going to take a miracle.

As we move closer to the gates, we all instinctually slow our pace, not wanting to look like warriors on a mission. The guards manning the gate notice us the moment they are in our visual range. As we get closer, I see smiles on their faces. At first, the fear that they might recognize us creeps into my mind, but after a few hundred more yards I can clearly see that they are staring at Tabitha, which turns my fear into rage. But I know that I must exercise discipline under these dire circumstances. The welcoming smiles of the fallen guards grow as we approach, and they open the pedestrian gate. We enter the search area one at a time. There are four of them, each carrying an assault rifle. The one who is in charge of this team speaks. "So, what business brings you all to this fine city?"

His gaze doesn't break contact with Tabitha's body. He looks her up and down as though she were a fresh meal. One of the other guards follows his lead, but the other two focus their attention on the rest of us. After a pause Tyrus answers the leader's question. "We're just here on routine business. Food vendor negotiations."

Tyrus breaks the leader's focus on Tabitha. He moves closer to Tyrus while looking each of us up and down.

"'Food vendor negotiations,' huh?" he says, mocking Tyrus.

"Why would four food distributors be dressed as soldiers? It would be my first time seeing that. And where are your transport vehicles? Food vendors don't just walk through the scorched third."

I can feel my body tensing up, ready to strike. I quickly make a plan on how I'm going to react—grabbing the rifle off the guard to my left, twisting it from his hands, and killing the man next to him. I'm hoping Alcyone, Sergios, and Tyrus will take care of the other two. I wait for Tyrus's lead to make a move.

Tyrus calmly answers the lead guard, "Well, our truck broke down in the middle of the dust, and we dress like this to discourage bandits from jumping us. We're hoping we can get a tow truck to go out there and bring us back in."

The lead guard looks intently at him, clearly not buying his story. He slowly looks over at Tabitha, smiles, and then looks back at Tyrus. "Tell you what, I don't really care what you're doing in this place. Hookers? Drugs? I get it. How 'bout you leave her with us and be on your way? Go ahead."

My blood is boiling, but I know I must wait for Tyrus's lead. None of us moves.

The lead man detects us stalling, so he grabs Tabitha by the arm and pulls her to the side. He quickly raises his rifle, pointing it at Tyrus. The guard next to him immediately follows suit and points his rifle at each of us in turn. The two guards behind them also point their rifles at us. This is it. We're done.

"Don't move!" the guard yells. The lead man looks annoyed and addresses Tyrus. "Well, you had your chance. I gave you a chance to go in, right? Now I think we'll just keep all of you here. We'll have more fun here anyway."

I decide that I'd rather go down fighting and slightly bend my knees, preparing to lunge. Before I can decide which guard to lunge at, the two guards in the rear drop their rifles, and faster than I can blink, each produces a thin metal wire from his sleeve. Before I can react to what's happening, they have the wires wrapped around the necks of the guards in front of them. I can see blood dripping from where the wires press into their skin as they claw at their necks, kicking, struggling, and gurgling on what I can only imagine is their own blood. I can see blood seeping into the whites of their eyes while the struggling slows and eventually stops. As the killers lower the bodies slowly to the ground, they look around to ensure no one has seen what just happened. Miraculously, no one has. We all stand still, jaws wide open in confusion at the violence we just witnessed.

The two guards quickly drop their murder weapons, pick up their rifles, and gesture for us to follow them through the next gate into the city. Having no choice but to trust them, we all follow. They casually walk up to the final gate that leads to the city. One of them waves at the guard in charge of final access control at the top of the lookout tower to open it. He routinely does it, paying us no mind. I am still in shock and confusion about what is happening. I want to ask some obvious questions, but it is clearly not the time. We follow the guards into the city and are thrown right into the hurried crowds. Each guard continually looks back to ensure they haven't lost us as we follow them to an unknown destination. They find an alley and quickly turn into it. Tyrus is the first to speak. "First of all, thank you both. But could you please shed some light on this situation?"

One of them answers, "We don't have much time before the rest of the fallen discover the dead men, but my name is Andel, and this is Alec. We are two of the forgotten. They thought they had cleared us of all memory of the savior, but we just played along, waiting for our time. We were both visited by angels last night in dreams, and both of us were given instructions about your coming. We've been expecting you." I can't believe it. "Now, Zypher and the others are being held at the end of the city at the top of an abandoned skyscraper. They're being pressed for information but haven't given the enemy anything useful yet. However, as you know, it's only a matter of time before one of them breaks. The two of us are the only resources you have in this city, so it's going to have to be the eight of us who conduct this mission. We can't fight the assigned fallen like you can, so we can take you only as far as the building. Then we are useless to you."

Tyrus knows we don't have time or options, so he looks at each of us to indicate this is going to happen, and it's going to happen now. His eyes land on me. "Lucien, you and Sergios go get some weapons while we work on the plan of attack."

"Yes, sir."

Sergios and I run out of the alley and retrieve what pistols we can from the first gun shop we see. Upon returning we find the rest of the team and the two double-agent guards eagerly awaiting us. Sergios and I pass out the cheap pistols we were able to find to the other members of the team. I hand one to Tabitha hesitantly, as I know she is not trained in 3D warfare. But I'd rather she have one than not have one. I'll just make sure to keep her behind me as we move.

"All right, let's move," orders Tyrus, with a hope in his voice I haven't heard since this mission began. We speed-walk our way through alleys and backstreets, following the two guards with complete trust that they know where our friends are being held. I have no problem trusting them, since what they have done would get them killed even if they weren't on our side. After about an hour of darting from alley to alley, I notice more and more abandoned buildings, see more and more dead, starved bodies, and recognize the gloom and lack of people that characterizes the edge of this terrible city. Andel and Alec pick up the pace, and we are running now. After about ten minutes, Andel motions for us to stop.

"Okay, the skyscraper is about a half mile up. The info we got says they are being held on the second from the top floor. Nothing works in these abandoned buildings, so we'll have to go right up the stairs. They are probably expecting this, so be ready."

Tyrus turns to an exhausted and bent-over Kratos. "All right, let's do it."

Kratos holds up his hand, signaling for a moment to catch his breath. Tyrus maintains his patience. After a minute or so, Kratos assigns each of us in turn. Andel and Alec have not been assigned angels, and we don't have time to train them in the ways of 4D fighting. They give us a look saying it is up to us now.

"We'll be here praying for you," says Andel.

Tyrus gives him a thankful nod and heads toward the building.

Our movements become stealthy now. The enemy more than likely knows a group of people have just been assigned angels near their position. As we get closer, I see what can only be the building Andel was talking about. It's about thirty stories high, covered in dust and grime. Most of its windows have been broken, and it looks like it's one gust of wind short of toppling over. It must have been the center of business in this area long ago before the city expanded to what it is now. We approach the building, and Tyrus tactically leads us around it, seeing if there is a back door we can enter. There are only double doors with shiny new chains locking them. The enemy has recently locked them. They know anyone coming on a rescue mission would be able to navigate such an obstacle, but they also know that to do so would cause quite a bit of noise, instantly giving away our position.

As all of this information runs through my head, Tyrus leaps in the air in front of one of the double doors and flies at it, shattering the chains. The crash echoes throughout the hollow streets, and we all know there is no point in being stealthy anymore. I get the familiar feeling that it is just too easy. Why aren't the perimeters being patrolled? They have to know we were coming. Is the squad even here? My trust in Andel and Alec is beginning to waver.

Tyrus rushes into the building through the broken doors, and the moment I lose sight of him there is a blinding explosion. It knocks all of us to the ground. I'm on my back, ears ringing and vision blurred. I still have enough wits about me to try to recover quickly, as an attack is sure to follow.

My first instinct is to check on Tabitha. I look around and see her lying unconscious on her side. Sprinting to her, I first check her vitals, which thankfully indicate she is alive.

At this point, I can hear bullets flying and hitting walls all around me. I want to stay with her, but I know I can't. I drag her behind a dumpster and find Kratos cowering in fear. I leave her there in the hopes the enemy won't find her. "Kratos! Watch her!"

I run into the fight. I can't even tell where the fire is coming from, so I take cover and try to regain my bearings. Looking around, I see Sergios on his back, unconscious and bleeding. Somehow Alcyone is returning fire at whatever is firing at us. I see him taking cover behind the corner of a nearby building and firing upward. Following the direction of his fire, all I can see is an empty window two stories up. I can only assume this is where the bullets are coming from, so I return fire with my pistol as well. After a few shots a body slumps over the window and slowly falls out, hitting the ground with a thud. It is an unassigned fallen. Alcyone and I meet eyes and nod to one another. He moves toward the building as I cover, and then he covers my movement. On the way, I drag Sergios inside the building, all the while remembering Tabitha where I left her. I fight away my feelings and start looking for Tyrus. Amidst the smoke I can't find him. I hear some coughing near me.

"*Tyrus?*" I yell.

A battered and bleeding Tyrus emerges from the smoke with a smile on his face.

"How did you—"

He cuts me off. "Can't kill me that easily."

He looks down at Sergios and notices his condition. He pulls a small vial out of his shirt pocket, opens it, and holds it to Sergios's nose. Sergios sits up quickly, eyes wide open.

"All right, so our cover is blown. Change of tactics," says Tyrus, the need for vengeance behind every word.

He runs down the hall, and we follow, guns drawn. He finds a staircase and sprints up it at full speed. I look up to see him charging through the air, meeting a demon head-on, producing the familiar shriek that I'll never get used to. I hear some footsteps behind me and charge right into a fallen assigned man, killing him instantly. Shrieks and collisions fill the next two minutes of exhausting combat. At one point, I tumble down the stairs after being hit from the side, but I remain assigned. My retaliation is quick and deadly.

We fight our way up two flights of stairs, leaving destroyed demons and fresh corpses in our wake. Although we are dominating the fight at this point, exhaustion is not far off and we cannot keep up this pace. I am drenched in sweat as I continue the fight. In the midst of hand-to-hand combat, I throw at least six men over the side of the staircase as I meet them along the way, sending them to their deaths. Bodies fall from above me as the rest of the team is victorious in fight after fight. I cannot breathe fast enough to supply my body with the oxygen it is demanding, but I am literally fighting for my life and the lives of my friends.

After dozens of flights of stairs and countless kills, there is a sudden lull in the action. We each collapse where we stand and breathe as hard and fast as men can, unable to talk. Tyrus, although exhausted, is the only one continuing to scan the area for more fallen. After a minute of recovery, he grabs each of us by the shirt, pulling us to our feet. The last thing I want is another fight, but I have to dig deeper than I ever have. Tyrus creeps up the stairs, pistol at the ready, eyes focused on what lies above.

We manage to make it to the second from the last floor, where Andel said the squad was being held. Tyrus continues upward. I tap him on the shoulder and point to the floor, indicating that we have made it to our intended destination. He motions for a huddle, and we all move in. He whispers, "We're gonna go in from the ceiling, guns blazing. Kill anyone who's not in the squad. Understand?"

We all nod.

He creeps his way up to the next floor. As we enter the door leading to the top floor of the building, I can see that it was clearly once the floor of executives. There are large offices with glass walls. The old, musty carpet is moist and smells of mildew. We slowly move our way from office to office, listening for signs of our friends below. Time and again Tyrus halts us so that he can listen more closely. After a few halts we hear nothing, as though we had killed everyone in the building. But then faint creaks from above can be heard. Tyrus gently lifts his head and looks up. He makes eye contact with each of us and points up. Perhaps the enemy moved the squad upon hearing the chaos of our entry.

Tyrus makes a series of gestures showing that he intends to bust through the ceiling. Our plan of attack remains the same, just from below instead of from above. We back up in a circle around him, ready to enter through the hole in the ceiling he is about to make. Before he can launch himself, shots are fired through the ceiling from above. Splinters of wood and bullets rain down on us while we run for cover. We don't return fire, as we don't want to hit members of the squad. Tyrus looks up in anger and flies through the ceiling, creating a gaping hole the size of a beach ball. We follow through the hole, and the fight is on.

When I reach the top of the building, the bullets are already flying and multiple collisions have already begun. For some odd reason no one is attacking me. After looking around for someone or something to fight, I realize I'm being of no help and run around the roof, looking for the squad. I find them behind a large generator, each tied to a chair, unassigned and bleeding. Although I can see the joy in their eyes for having seen me, their brokenness, physically and spiritually, is apparent. I pull out a knife and quickly cut each of them loose. I get to Zypher and can see that he has been tortured the worst. He is missing a couple fingers, and one of his eyes has been gouged out. It stabs me in the heart to see my leader in this condition. He looks at me with his one eye and nods in gratitude. *How is it that I am saving such a man as Zypher?* The sheer irony of the situation seems unreal to me.

None of these men can help us, so I return to the fight. I return to the chaos to see dozens of dead fallen men lying on the ground. There are so many of them that the team is beginning to trip over them in the middle of the fighting. I am immediately put in a choke hold from behind by an unassigned fallen, and I easily throw him over the side of the building. A few more collisions, and I am again exhausted, completely unable to fight. Luckily, every man guarding the squad has fled or been killed. I look around to see the team spent. We have never had to fight so much in such a little amount of time. Zypher and the squad limp their way to our position. Zypher and Tyrus meet eyes. Zypher is the first to speak. "Guess you had nothing better to do, huh?"

"Well, sir, I didn't want the responsibility of babysitting these turds anymore, so I had to come back for you."

I can see the pain in Tyrus's eyes at seeing Zypher so broken. But it doesn't cover the joy he has for the fact that he is still alive. They share a weak chuckle and embrace. Tyrus allows for short reunions among members of the newly complete squad, but then he urges us all to move. We obey and make our way back down the stairs.

"I saw a good number of the fallen take off with their tails between their legs, so you can be sure they will return with reinforcements. We're going to have to breach the edge of the city on its east side and go around in the dust," says Zypher to Tyrus.

Tyrus nods in agreement. As we hurry down the stairs as fast as the injured men can move, I hear someone running up the stairs from below. We all brace for what we hope is not a large number of fallen. We approach the door that leads down to the next staircase and stack up, ready to attack once more. I am in the lead and kick the door open, pistol at the ready. I am met face-to-face with a glowing Tabitha, who is also ready to charge. We pause for a half second in shock and immediately embrace.

"I'm so sorry I left you there." I hold her tightly.

"You did what you had to do. It's okay."

Our hug lasts longer than Tyrus is willing to wait. "Okay, lovebirds, let's get moving!"

We break away from each other and continue running down the stairs. Time and again injured men from the rescued squad stumble out of weakness and we have to help them to their feet. I hate to even imagine what they've been subjected to, but we have to keep moving, or we're all dead.

We finally reach the bottom floor, and as we make our way toward the exit, I suddenly remember that Kratos is not with us. We stack up on the exit and kick the door open, only to find Kratos smoking a cigarette while leaning against the side of the building. He's still alive.

"Took you ladies long enough. I was really getting bored down here."

Tyrus looks at him for a second as I wait for his built-up anger against Kratos to finally be unleashed. To my surprise, he just smiles and puts his arm roughly around Kratos, rubbing his knuckle into his head. Everyone is so broken, assigning them would be useless. Besides, urgency is paramount.

We tactically make our way east, into even darker and fouler parts of the city. The smell of rotting flesh grows stronger as more and more corpses litter the streets. The desperate, starving people with no hope or strength to even participate in cannibalism have come out here to die. I try my best not to look on the hopeless expressions frozen on each corpse: a true and complete surrender to despair. I will never forget these faces.

Although we are most likely being pursued by the enemy, I can't stop my heart from hurting for these people. I picture what their ends must have been like and where their souls reside now. How did they end up in Babylon? What were the dreams that led them here?

We continue quietly moving from alley to alley, street to street. From a distance an awful moaning can be heard. As we move farther east, it gets louder and louder. It pierces my ears and tears through my soul. I know it is the sound of someone knocking at death's door. I can't bear it. We approach an open main road, and I can see something moving on the ground. I focus my eyes on what it is, and I can make out in the faded moonlight that it is a woman crawling slowly on the ground, using her arms to drag herself an inch at a time toward only she knows what. Every movement is accompanied by a weak moan of ultimate suffering.

Unable to think logically, I run toward her. The sounds of my footsteps cause her to slowly turn and look up at me. Her eyes are wide and large. Her expression is vacant. Her blond hair has mostly fallen out, and her cheeks are sunk in so deep I can see the outline of her jawbone. Her once fancy clothes have become tattered rags that hang off of her emaciated body. I am too shocked to move. I can see every major bone in her body, her pale, paper-thin flesh clinging to each one. With what strength she can muster she grabs at my legs, pulling at my pant leg. I can only interpret this as a gesture of desperation that begs for rescue from the hell that being alive is for her. I snap out of my shock, pull out my canteen, and quickly open it to give her water. A harsh, sharp whisper hits me from behind. *"What are you doing? Get up! We have to move!"*

It's Tyrus. For the first time since being a part of this squad, I disobey orders. Pouring water into this woman's dry mouth is the only thing I can do to ease my own distress. She is able to drink only a portion of it, as her mouth and tongue are weak and dried out. Tyrus grabs me by the collar, pulling me to my feet. Instinctually, I push him off me. Pausing in shock, I realize what I have just done. The look he gives me is not what I am anticipating. He knows that my empathy is the only reason for my rebellion. He takes a moment to consider, looks back, and slowly walks toward me with a surrendered posture. Bending down toward the dying woman, he gently lifts her over his shoulder and stands, looking at me. We both know that this may cause loss of life in our squad, but he has clearly decided to have pity not only on this poor woman, but on me as well. He looks back at the squad. "All right, let's move!"

After another hour or so of silent, tactical movement, we reach the edge of the city. The east side of the city is bordered by a huge cement wall, about two hundred feet high. It almost resembles a castle wall and appears impassable. Alcyone and Sergios take cover and face west, while Tyrus hands me the woman he's had on his shoulder for the last hour.

I can feel her faint breathing on my shoulder, indicating she is still alive. I set her gently against the wall and give her more water. She looks at me like a baby looks at its mother. Tyrus moves slowly in front of the wall, pressing his ear against it at different points. I'm not sure what he's listening for, but he finds a spot. I see him back up, glow brighter, and rise into the air. I brace for the impact. What sounds like two big rigs colliding echoes throughout the city. When the dust clears, I can see that only about a six-inch indent has been created in the wall. Tyrus charges up and repeats his assault on the wall. After a few more violent collisions, he is making some progress. I continue nourishing the woman and can see her mouth and tongue beginning to move more freely as she becomes hydrated. After each collision I look back, sure that the entire city can hear the dismantling of this great wall. After yet another earth-shattering collision, I look back, see nothing, and return my attention to the woman. At that moment several bullets hit the wall right next to her head. They have found us. Not thinking of her fragility, I throw her over my shoulder and run for cover.

"Buy me some time, gents!" yells Tyrus right before he launches himself into the wall yet again.

I leave the woman behind a building where I hope she will survive. Bullets fly, and collision after collision is followed by the shriek of defeated demons. We are severely outnumbered and cannot possibly kill all of these fallen. As we kill them, they only seem to multiply, coming in waves from the west.

"Okay! Breach is open!" I hear Tyrus yell from behind me. We make a tactical retreat, bullets flying over our heads and flying demons just missing us, colliding with buildings and making craters in the ground. I manage to find the woman I was helping, throw her over my shoulder, and charge for the small hole in the wall that Tyrus has made. In a single-file line we all run out into the dust. We are met by a violent dust storm. This seems to be only salt on the wounds and horrors we have all just survived. When the last of us is out, Tyrus charges the wall from the outside just above the hole, causing it to collapse on itself. The falling rubble crushes a few fallen men who were following us through the hole in the wall. I can see blood seeping through the bottom of the rubble as I look back, running as fast as my exhaustion will allow.

We regroup just outside the wall while Tyrus counts us, ensuring we have everyone. We do. It takes a minute, as it is difficult to see through the dust that fills the air. I can see we are nothing but exhausted and injured. I think we made it out just in time, as there isn't much, if any, fight left in any of us.

But we must move.

Tyrus leads us out into the storm. The wind is too loud to hear his voice, so he's using hand motions. We head farther east, which seems counterproductive, but I quickly conclude that hugging the city's borders would only get us killed, so we must make a huge loop around the city farther out than the fallen would ever search.

After several hours, the storm subsides and Tyrus halts the formation. I look behind us and realize that the storm was a blessing in disguise. Had it been calm, the fallen could have easily tracked our footsteps in the dust, but now there is no trace of which direction we headed to or came from. I can see Tyrus relax in the knowledge that we are, at least for the time being, safe from harm.

"All right, gents, take some time to rest while you can."

CHAPTER

BURDENS

ost of the group fall into the dust where they stand, each gasping for breath looking into the brown sky. With what gentleness I can muster, I set the woman I am carrying into the dust on her back. Her face is caked in dust, and I do my best to clean it off with water. The shock of the cold water causes her to struggle a bit. I am happy to see some life in her. Although I am desperate for water, I make sure she gets plenty first. In an instant Tabitha is by my side, kneeling next to me and offering the woman a pouch of food paste. Just the smell of it causes her to sit up and grab it from Tabitha's hand. As she eats, Tabitha gently rubs her shoulder. She is indifferent to it. After a few bites of food she looks at Tabitha and me in turn, clearly confused as to why anyone would help her. It breaks my heart to realize that kindness has become a foreign language to this broken woman, but I am happy to offer her some relief from suffering. Looking over at Tabitha, I can see she carries the same hurt for having realized this. I think Tabitha holds more empathy for this woman than I do. Looking unsure of what she is about to say, she gently speaks to the woman. "What's your name?"

The woman slowly stops eating and looks at us in fear, as though sharing that information would be giving away some dark secret. She looks down at her food and then back at us. "Antheia."

Upon saying this, she searches our reactions, unsure how we will respond. We both smile. This seems to put her at ease enough to continue eating. We leave her to her food, not wanting to press her further. I look to Tabitha and firmly embrace her, letting her know how relieved I am that she is okay. As I release my hold, she doesn't let me go. I can tell this experience has taken its toll on her, so I hold her until I know she feels safe. She finally releases her embrace and sits next to the woman. Even though she is in need of comfort, she would rather offer it to someone in greater need. Moments like these only increase my growing love for the beautiful woman that Tabitha is.

I leave them alone and walk around, checking on the men. Most of them are fast asleep; some are eating and joking with one another, grateful for what can only have been divine intervention that allowed us to escape. I can see just outside of the group that Zypher is sitting by himself, a peaceful look on his face as he stares out into the calm night. Slowly, I approach to see if I might be invited to join him. He looks up at me, smiling like an honored father. "Sit down, killer."

I gladly take the invitation. We stare into the night together in silence. I've noticed that the ability to be at peace following chaos and turmoil increases with more battles fought. When you rarely have time for true rest, you learn to take full advantage of any opportunity for it. After a few minutes, Zypher reaches his arm around my shoulder and gives me a fatherly shake. This simple gesture makes me feel as though I just slayed a dragon.

"You know, Lucien, pressure and trial are what reveal a man's true character. I've seen you time and again in the fight show what kind of man you really are. I have to say, it makes me proud to have met you."

These words sting. I am honored to hear them from such a great man, but I don't believe them. Regardless of what good I may have done, I still feel weak and insecure. I have no issue with revealing my true heart to Zypher, so I tell him what's hidden in this raw moment. "I'm so afraid. I can never get used to suffering or the fear that there is only more to come. I don't know what's wrong with me. I don't believe God meant for us to live in this kind of fear, but I can't shake it."

He pauses with a nostalgic smile.

"Believe me, I know exactly how you feel." I think it is the first time he has ever smiled at me. "I spent most of my life feeling incapable, weak, broken, and unworthy. Lucien, it's only in that kind of despair that we learn our true need for the savior. If we were completely capable and confident men, what need would we have for Him?"

"Okay, so if I recognize my need for Him, then where is He?" I choke on my own cynicism.

"Suffering has an awful way of making Him seem invisible. And I know you've heard a thousand times that He is closest to us in our need and pains, but it's true. It's in our suffering that we grow closest to Him. It's also during these times that some of our most heroic deeds are done." I look up at his face and consider the meaning of his words as I stare at the hole in his face where his eye used to be. "No one ever said doing good always *feels* good. As a matter of fact, it usually doesn't. That's what makes it heroic. As fallen sinners our tendencies are to do only what feels good. If doing God's will always felt great, everyone would do it, thereby negating what makes it selfless. The risk and sacrifice you just took probably was marked with fear, uncertainty, and pain, but you did it anyway. That's what I mean by saying that your true character is being revealed. Do you think Jesus was at peace in the garden of Gethsemane? Do you think the cross felt good for him? But look at the result. True love is defined by sacrifice."

His words make sense but don't take away my pain.

"So how do I escape this suffering?"

"You're asking the wrong question, Lucien. It's not about escaping or not escaping it. Life in this fallen world is full of suffering, believer or not. What makes us different is what we do in our suffering and the result of it. The poor souls you saw running around Babylon are all looking for an escape from what pains them. They truly believe that if they just made a little more money, if they just had more of a sexual connection with their next partner, if they just had a better car, then their pain would end. They are working toward an end by means of a road that is a true dead end, and that is a tragedy. We are working toward a savior that is the only cure to every pain that has ever existed. If He gave us a quick cure, then we wouldn't need to constantly be seeking Him. And think of this: without suffering we would be much more susceptible to believing the lie that something in this world, be it marriage or success or whatever, is the cure."

I sit silently, pondering his words and allowing them to sink in. I am frustrated to conclude that he is right. Although Zypher being right means that my relationship with the savior will only become richer, it also means that suffering may have to continue. In this moment, I think of Paul rejoicing while he is in chains. I think it is this kind of peace that I long for. Perhaps asking the wrong questions has prevented me from experiencing that peace. I'm filled with mixed emotions, and I don't know what to say.

Zypher sees my struggle and continues, "Hey, don't try to figure it all out right now. Just start asking the right questions, and keep seeking Him. You've been through a lot, and I just want to say again how proud of you I am. I also want to thank you for saving my life."

I look over at him in confusion, not feeling like I saved his life but that I only took a small part in the mission that Tyrus led, which did save his life. He slaps me on the shoulder with a parting smile. "Get some rest, killer."

He leaves me alone with my thoughts. As I stare into the endless night, my eyelids become heavy. Exhaustion is setting in, and I must rest. Lying on my side in the dust, I fade into my dream world, hoping for some peace there.

The next moment, I find myself being stung with overwhelmingly cold wind and beaten down with heavy rainfall. Looking around, I see nothing but waves, clouds, and lightning. I am standing in the middle of an old wooden ship, surrounded by a raging storm. Frantically looking in all directions to see if I can find land, panic grows as I can see nothing but tormented sea. I am so cold that my body is shaking uncontrollably, making it difficult to even walk, not to mention the effect of the rocking ship. I feel as though I will be tossed overboard at any moment. I have never been at sea, but it suddenly occurs to me to search for an anchor so that I can throw it overboard.

Trembling from the vicious cold and running about the upper deck of the ship, I find nothing. I search for any passage that might lead to a lower deck, but I find nothing. I can hear the hull of the old ship cracking as each wave collides with it. I am trapped and helpless, at the mercy of the storm. I drop to my knees and cry out for mercy.

"Where are you?"

Nothing.

"You always leave me like this! *Why won't you just let me die here? I give up, okay? Is that what you want?"*

Tears and trembling accompany my words. I have no more strength to yell or fight, or even to hope. He has left me and is never coming back. I will never understand His absence in such suffering. I will never know where He is or why He has left. I will die here, alone and without any explanation. I lie down and surrender to my fate. My eyes close as the unrelenting rain beats down on my shivering body. Please just let me die. Let me die.

At the moment of surrender a gentle voice surprises me. "Giving up already? It's just a little rain."

Opening my eyes, I look up to see Octavian. He reaches down, offering me his hand. He is a small sign that I may make it out of here. I take his hand, and he pulls me to my feet.

"Of course you'll make it out of this, you drama queen. Why do you always assume the moment pain arrives that you have been abandoned? How many times do I have to tell you that He will never leave you?"

"But it feels so much like He's gone."

He chuckles at my answer.

"You humans and your feelings. How is it that you can master any subject in only eight years of schooling but spend a lifetime remaining emotional children?" The rain drips off his nose and chin. "The Father has told you, through His word and even through me, an angel, that He will never leave you or forsake you. How can simple feelings make you disbelieve that? Lucien, this is all part of growing up, my friend. How does a child ever become a man without trials and having to trust during those trials? Look around you."

I wipe the water off my face and try to see. The rain is still blinding, but I begin to feel every lightning bolt and gale of wind as though it were cutting my heart. The rain feels like it is beating down on my soul, as though sorrow had physical weight to it. The waves that crash about and against one another feel like chaos in my mind as I watch them break apart against each other.

"That's right, Lucien. What haunts you underneath any happiness that may come and go is before you. It's why your stomach hurts for apparently no reason. What you see is the leftover pain of all the suffering you have witnessed, all the sins you have committed that you can't forgive yourself for, the love you have lost, and the dreams you have hoped for that never came true."

He looks over at me slowly and nods slightly, as though I know what he's about to say. And I do know.

"Who is the only one who can calm any storm, Lucien?"

I don't want to say it, because I know and have known the answer to that question my entire life. "Lucien ..."

My trembling lips open, and the name comes out like a breath of life. "Jesus."

Octavian smiles as I look up at him. As his smile grows, the rain subsides and I can see every youthful feature of his face revealed by life-giving sunshine. The sea around us calms, and its surface looks like glass. The boat is still, the clouds are gone, and the sky is the brightest blue I have ever seen.

"The Bible ain't kidding when it says there is power in His name." He takes a deep breath. "Now, I know what you're thinking, buddy: *Why didn't He just do this earlier?* Right? Well, how strong would your faith be, how memorable would His comfort be, and how much would you know your true need for Him if He just took all your pain away the instant it appeared? There is more horrific evil attacking you than you can even imagine. The pain He has allowed you to experience is just a taste of what the enemy intends. It's all for His good and for yours. He is preparing you for eternity. Do yourself a favor, and stop giving absolute power to your feelings. To surrender to despair is to lose faith in the one who is holding you through it. It's not that He's going to catch you as you fall. It's that He's been holding you the whole time. You're okay, little buddy. And whether your earthly body is destroyed in this righteous fight or you die of ripe old age, you're His, forever and beyond. You will never in all eternity have to fight a battle without Him right beside you."

I am immediately ashamed of my lack of faith and weakness.

"Stop it! Stop with the shame, stop with the beating yourself down, stop with the guilt! It's over, Lucien. He took it all, and you can let go and be free of all that. Do you think He wants you to live like that? You do it to yourself. The only person who needs to forgive you now is you. Let ... it ... go."

I look at him again, and as our eyes meet I can feel that every word he has said is absolutely and completely true. As the tears fall, I nod my head and open my heart. For the first time I am letting God do His work. I have been fighting Him for so long, hanging on to pain and confusion. It is finally time to let it all go. I have wandered in the desert for far too long, and I can't take another minute of it. Why have I not just surrendered to His embrace when He has been there waiting for me the whole time? Peace and joy awaited me, but I chose despair and misery. Why? Now I know why. I didn't feel worthy of it. How could I deserve such forgiveness and love? How would it ever be right if someone like me had been restored and given true love, wiped clean of all wrongdoing? Octavian grabs my shoulder and gently shakes me.

"Now you finally get it. Light is being shed on the true reality of what grace means. You *don't* deserve it. You *aren't* worthy. No one is, buddy. Why do you think Jesus died on that terrible cross? I know you logically know the answer, but your heart is finally starting to grasp it. Your freedom is a gift. You didn't, nor could you ever, earn it. All sinners deserve to be away from Him for all eternity. But He took all your punishment so He could spend eternity with you. *That's* how much He loves you."

I feel the warmth of the sun soothing my skin. Octavian continues, "Have you ever thought about what God was doing in the very beginning, before sin entered the world? He simply spent the days with Adam and Eve, walking with them in the garden. That was what He always wanted from the beginning. Just to be with you. And when Satan corrupted that, He took every measure necessary to ensure that things would return to that state, even though it took Him having to go through the worst and most terrible suffering that has ever been experienced by any being in existence."

No truth has ever hit me as hard as this realization. It is overwhelming in every joyous and victorious way that can be experienced. My knees become weak, and I slowly sit on the ship's deck. Peace envelopes every part of my being, washing away all hopelessness, pain, and any memory of my sins. My eyes gently close as I bask in this unfamiliar peace. I can feel my whole body warm up from the inside out, and the gentle touch of a hand on my cheek. I can't place why, but I know it's not Octavian's. My eyes want to open to see who it is, but I can't bring myself to do it. And I know there is no need to open my eyes, because I know who it is. Fading into peace beyond description, I lose consciousness.

My eyes slowly open, but there is no pain in my stomach, which makes me think I am still dreaming. Slowly looking around, I see figures lying in the dust, and the familiar brown sky. Only this time I don't feel as though I'm waking to a nightmare of a reality. I am fully aware of the dire situation in which I now live, and the missions and battles that may lie ahead, but I accept them all. I never knew what it meant to have true, biblical peace until now. There is not even fear that it will go away, which is what usually has accompanied happiness in the past. This kind of peace is pure. I know I will most likely experience suffering again before leaving the Earth, but I'm somehow not afraid of it anymore.

This is a miracle.

Am I even myself anymore? Or perhaps I am more of myself than I have ever been. It is what freedom feels like. It is what being consumed by love feels like. It's not even a feeling; it's a state of being.

My vision has changed. As the people from the squad get up, there is genuine empathy in my heart with what they must be feeling and what may be going through their minds. I know I've always had this kind of empathy, but now it's uninterrupted by my own trouble, as though someone had tuned my radio station to eliminate all static. I want to speak with all of them to see what I can do to help their day be brighter.

Naturally, I go to Tabitha first. She is in a deep sleep when I find her, wrapped up in her sleep sack like it's a cocoon. Only the top of her face is exposed, from the bridge of her nose and up. Seeing her sleep in peace makes me feel guilty to have to wake her. I bend down and gently stroke the top of her head. Her face emerges from under its warm covering, and I see a smile grow. She slowly pulls one of her arms free and caresses my other hand as I continue petting her little head. Her eyes remain closed, but she knows it's me.

"Hey, dork." She reaches up and lightly touches my face.

"Hey, you. Did you have good dreams?"

She opens her eyes and just smiles and nods.

"Well, maybe someday you can tell me about them."

"Maybe."

How she maintains such peace through all this is something I may finally understand. She understood long before me what it means to completely surrender to the savior and just trust Him. For the first time her source of strength is no longer a mystery to me. Had I known of this before, I could have saved myself so much misery. However, I suppose without the misery I would never have arrived at such peace. This truth leads me to wonder if Tabitha has taken a similar path in her journey. But this moment is one I'd rather not disturb with stories of pain and struggles.

Before I have a chance to say another word, a deafening boom knocks me to the ground. Lying face down in the dust, I hear nothing. All I can think of is whether Tabitha is all right or not. The need to protect her overcomes my stunned state, and I leap to my feet. Looking around, I cannot find her. I only see her empty sleep sack lying on the ground. As my hearing begins to return, the sounds of collisions and shrieks surround me. Where is Tabitha? Pushing aside my duty to fight, I run around in disarray and panic. An overwhelming force takes me off my feet and puts me in the dust once again.

Blood now drips from my head, soaking into the ground. The dull red color of my blood tells me I that I am now unassigned. Vulnerability and fear are all that I feel now. Collision after collision pierces my eardrums. Finding Tabitha is my only thought. Standing awakens an unbearable pain in my left leg, and I collapse. My femur has been shattered. All I can do is wail in agony. After wiping the pouring blood from my brow, my eyes meet Tabitha's. She is lying on her side in the dust, unassigned and bleeding from multiple wounds on her face. There is nothing I can do.

A black swirl of evil becomes a lifeless face, hovering above her. Her hand weakly reaches toward me, shaking, as her eyes reach out to me with a desperate plea for rescue. The demon delivers its final blow, crushing Tabitha's broken body. As the dust clears, I see her. Her eyes are open, but there is no more life in them. Her executioner now hovers above me. I look the demon deep into its hideous eyes.

"Do it," I plead. A smile now grows on the demon's face as it basks in the misery of my plea for death.

"Please do it."

I want nothing more than to go home.

Made in the USA
Las Vegas, NV
04 March 2022

44992533R00106